"What I want to kn...
think I'm some sort of serial killer."

"Before I answer that, tell me about your conviction. Who did you murder?"

He clenched his jaw and sat back. Pain jackknifed through his heart as memories of the past bombarded him. Usually he managed to keep it bottled up. It was the only way he'd survived this long. But that one simple question—who did you murder?—coming from this pretty, young agent who reminded him far too much of another woman he'd once loved had the wound in his soul splitting open again.

"Mr. O'Brien? Who did you kill?"

If it wasn't for his terms of parole, he'd tell her exactly what he thought of her callous question. But she was in law enforcement. He had to cooperate or face the consequences.

"Who did I kill, Special Agent Malone?" He cleared his throat, trying to keep the bile down even though he felt like throwing up. "I killed my wife."

HUNTING THE CROSSBOW KILLER

LENA DIAZ

Harlequin
INTRIGUE

Sending thanks to my sister, Laura Brown, for telling me about the mysterious Lake Lanier that gave me the idea for this series. The inspiration for this particular book in the series was the emotional, heart-tugging song "Bobby" by Reba McEntire.

Harlequin® INTRIGUE™

Recycling programs for this product may not exist in your area.

ISBN-13: 978-1-335-45733-2

Hunting the Crossbow Killer

Copyright © 2025 by Lena Diaz

Harlequin Enterprises ULC
22 Adelaide St. West, 41st Floor
Toronto, Ontario M5H 4E3, Canada
www.Harlequin.com

Printed in Lithuania

MIX
Paper | Supporting responsible forestry
FSC® C021394

Lena Diaz was born in Kentucky and has also lived in California, Louisiana and Florida, where she now resides with her husband and two children. Before becoming a romantic suspense author, she was a computer programmer. A Romance Writers of America Golden Heart® Award finalist, she has also won the prestigious Daphne du Maurier Award for Excellence in Mystery/Suspense. To get the latest news about Lena, please visit her website, lenadiaz.com.

Books by Lena Diaz

Harlequin Intrigue

A Mystic Lake Mystery

Hunting the Crossbow Killer

A Tennessee Cold Case Story

Murder on Prescott Mountain
Serial Slayer Cold Case
Shrouded in the Smokies
The Secret She Keeps
Smoky Mountains Graveyard

The Justice Seekers

Cowboy Under Fire
Agent Under Siege
Killer Conspiracy
Deadly Double-Cross

Visit the Author Profile page at Harlequin.com.

CAST OF CHARACTERS

Aidan O'Brien—He spent ten years in prison for the "mercy" killing of his wife. But did he really kill her? Or did someone frame him and is now trying to silence him before the truth comes out?

Grace Malone—This newly minted FBI special agent is looking into whether a recent incident in Mystic Lake was done by the Crossbow Killer or a copycat. But first she has to find out the truth about her primary suspect. Is Aidan the killer she's after? Or is he being set up, both today and years ago in the death of his wife?

Mystic Lake Police Department—Police Chief Beau Dawson and his three-person crew focus their efforts on proving that Aidan O'Brien is responsible for a recent attempted murder.

Stella Holman—She runs the town's only bed-and-breakfast. She's also one of Aidan's only friends in Mystic Lake. Their secret history together could be the key to discovering whether Aidan is the killer terrorizing the town.

Billy Thompson—Owner of the marina and a retired military pilot, he also flies the town's medevac. But when disaster strikes, his role becomes the focus of Grace's investigation.

Chapter One

Grace paused on the brick-paved sidewalk, subtly smoothing her hand down her light jacket to make sure her pistol
was still secure in her shoulder holster and out of sight. Just
steps away was a narrow cobblestoned street. The street
was deserted at the moment, likely because most of the
people were attending the fall festival on the other side of
the lake that split the town in two.

The sun had risen over the Smoky Mountains hours ago,
but its rays were only just now beginning to penetrate the
thick woods surrounding the town and burn off the mist
rising from the water, partially obscuring the clusters of
boats bobbing up and down.

The locals had dubbed this isolated Tennessee mountain
town Mystic Lake, both for the lake of the same name and
for its mysterious origins. Over seventy years ago, a series
of unprecedented superstorms had dumped so much water
on the mountains that mudslides had diverted a nearby river
permanently. The resulting flash flood submerged a tiny
logging town whose name had long since been forgotten,
tragically drowning most of the residents. Those who'd survived never got the chance to retrieve their dead or rebuild

what they'd once had. With the river now feeding the new lake, the water never receded.

This new town had gradually emerged. But as time went by, an alarming number of mysterious deaths and disappearances began to occur in the area. Speculation was that the original people who were killed when the lake covered the logging town were now haunting the area, reaching up from the lake's murky depths to punish those who dared to claim the land or drive boats over their watery graves. The lake was eerie, oppressive, dangerous. Or, at least, that was what Grace had read on the internet. Reality was proving to be something else entirely. Mystic Lake, both the water and the town, was beautiful, enchanting and compelling.

The festival appeared to be in full swing now with people milling around colorful tents set up in front of the town's only bed-and-breakfast and a couple of homegrown restaurants. Some of those tents no doubt held musicians, because Grace could hear the faint notes of a haunting melody drifting across the water.

Children laughed and played on slides and swings in a park at the end of the street. But a petting zoo just past the park appeared to be the largest attraction for families. A menagerie of farm animals bleated, mooed or clucked as they mingled with the townspeople behind a temporary rope fence that had been set up. And just to the left of that was a sloping hill where the lake and town both ended and thick woods began.

Towering oak, ash and hemlock trees in varying shades of green covered the mountains. Giant swaths of maples created a gorgeous sweep of oranges and yellows across the lower elevations, their leaves just starting to turn. It was as if an artist had purposely planted them so their leaves would flicker like brilliant flames as autumn descended. A few weeks from now, maybe even a month, this place would be bustling with tourists. Leaf peepers would brave the town's ominous reputation and take the hour-long drive down the winding two-lane road that was the only way in or out so they could witness nature's fiery display. But Grace was no tourist. And she wasn't here to soak in the sights or even partake in the festival.

Turning around, she studied the long row of fanciful-looking shops and businesses that bordered the sidewalk on her side of the lake, searching for one in particular. Would it be covered in stone and ivy like some of these buildings? Or was it one of the wooden structures with whitewashed cedar shakes and colorful wood trim gleaming brightly in the sunlight? The only thing for certain was that it would have flowers in front. All of the buildings did. Pink and white spilled over the sides of window boxes or filled large terra-cotta pots, whimsical like the cover of a book of fairy tales. But that fairy tale exterior could very well be hiding something dark and twisted, an evil that no one suspected was living here among them.

No one, that is, except Grace.

She continued down the sidewalk, noting the names of each shop or business as she passed. When she found the one she was looking for, she pulled on the door, nearly running into it when it didn't open as she'd expected. Frowning, she pushed, in case the door swung in instead of out. It didn't budge. It was locked.

Cupping her hands against the dark tinted window, she peered inside. Sure enough, there wasn't anyone sitting at the small cluster of desks. There was a glass-enclosed conference room on the back wall that was obviously empty.

And the other areas she noted were empty, as well. But there were two doors on the left wall that were closed. Maybe someone was behind them. She knocked. When nothing happened, she knocked louder. Still nothing. She sighed and shook her head. They must have closed for the festival. Unbelievable. What kind of police department locked up the building and didn't leave at least one officer to handle emergencies? She'd have to go find them.

She whirled around and stepped onto the sidewalk.

"Ooof," she muttered as a man slammed into her.

He grabbed her around her waist, saving her from what would have been a nasty fall on the brick sidewalk. As soon as she was steady on her feet, he dropped his hands and hastily moved back.

"Sorry, ma'am. You okay?"

The slight Irish brogue in his deep voice had her looking up at him, her face heating with embarrassment over her clumsiness. Good grief, he was tall, and buff from the looks of his broad shoulders and the way his denim jacket tapered at his narrow waist cupped by faded jeans. But it was his face that had her cheeks heating even more. There was no other word to describe it except beautiful, like an angel's might be. His angular, sculpted cheeks were kissed by the sun, his skin a golden color that gave way to a barely-there beard and mustache. Wavy brown hair was just long enough to look in need of a cut and to save him from total perfection.

Then she met his gaze.

Grace had to suppress a shiver. His eyes were so dark they were almost black, with shadows seeming to swirl in their depths, giving him a sad, tortured look that hinted at mysterious secrets that took him from angel to fallen angel.

Her face heated even more as she realized she was staring. She cleared her throat and held out her hand to shake. "Sorry about that. I didn't look before I stepped onto the sidewalk. I'm Grace—"

Ignoring her hand, he circled around her and strode away at a brisk pace.

She blinked, her embarrassment giving way to annoyance. "Nice to meet you, too," she muttered as she straightened her jacket, automatically checking her weapon again and smoothing her hands down her slacks.

After giving one last frowning glance at the darkened building behind her, she headed in the same direction as the fallen angel, who was already heading around the end of the lake toward the other side. But something, or someone, must have caught his attention, because he abruptly changed direction and started up the hill toward the woods.

Near the tree line he stopped and sat in the shade of a maple tree, knees drawn up, his hands clasped across them. He was too far away for Grace to see his expression, but his posture seemed tense, like a bird of prey ready to swoop down or maybe fly away. The question was which would he do? And why were the few other townspeople on the same hill giving him wary looks and moving away?

Grace added him to the top of her list of people to speak to while she was here. Well, not the very top, but second for sure. The first person she had to speak to was no doubt somewhere in the crowd by the tents.

As she rounded the end of the lake and started across the bottom of the sloping hill, she spotted the man she was looking for, as evidenced by the flash of sun on the old-fashioned gold star on his uniform. She supposed he could be one of the regular police officers instead of the chief. But she doubted it. Confidence and authority seemed to surround him like an aura. The townspeople gave him the deference and respect that one would expect of someone in his position, politely smiling and greeting him as they passed.

Before approaching him, she couldn't resist one quick glance up at the morose stranger she'd run into earlier. He was still in the same spot, but this time she was close enough to make out his expression. His mouth was drawn into a tight line of displeasure. And as she followed the direction of his gaze, she realized it was focused on the same group of people she was approaching, the one that included the police chief.

She started to make her way through the small crowd to introduce herself to the chief when something whizzed through the air just past her toward the lake. Someone screamed. Grace blinked in shock when she saw a large white feather on the haft of an arrow sticking out of the side of one of the small boats docked near the shore.

Chaos erupted as some people fled and others swarmed the boat, checking on the two people inside. The police chief shouted orders. Two officers emerged from the crowd and began moving people back. The chief sprinted toward the hill, charging past her. She whirled around just in time to see the fallen angel disappearing into the woods with the chief in pursuit.

Grace wanted to rush after him to provide backup, but she was more worried about the safety of the people on the hill. There didn't seem to be enough police officers for crowd control, so she sprinted up the hill herself, directing the few families and children there to move away from the woods and down toward the cover of the tents and playground area.

Once everyone was safe, she headed toward the dock, ready to offer medical assistance if needed. But it didn't seem that anyone had been injured. Another officer appeared from around a group of people and motioned to one of the two by the boat. Together, he and that officer headed up the hill where the stranger and the chief had disappeared.

With everything under control now with the townspeople, Grace decided it was time to join the police. There was no such thing as too much backup.

She jogged up the hill but stopped when one of the officers stepped out from the trees carrying a crossbow and a quiver of arrows, each one bearing a long white feather on the end.

Grace's breath caught when she noted the bloodred line painted down the center of each feather. She swallowed, hard, as the police chief emerged from the woods a few feet away leading a man in handcuffs. The fallen angel.

His tortured, angry gaze met hers and she couldn't help but wonder if she was looking into the eyes of the man she'd come here to find.

The serial killer known as the *Crossbow Killer*.

Chapter Two

Grace tugged on the door to the police station, relieved when it opened this time. A quick glance to her right reassured her that the suspect was sitting in the holding cell that she'd seen earlier when peeking through the window. He glanced at her, then quickly looked away.

"May I help you, ma'am?" The smiling young officer who'd been carrying the bow and arrows earlier had been sitting at one of the desks when she'd stepped inside. Now he was walking toward her, stopping a few feet away. "You were on the hill when we brought out Mr. O'Brien, right?"

"O'Brien? That's the man who was handcuffed?"

His smile dimmed, as if he realized he'd shared information that he probably shouldn't have. "I'm Officer Danny Ortiz. You don't appear to be from around here. I know pretty much everyone in town by sight, if not by name. And the tourists haven't invaded quite yet this fall."

"You're right. I'm not from around here." She hesitated, preferring to introduce herself to his boss first. "I was hoping to speak to the chief. On the front door it says his name is Beau Dawson."

He nodded, his dark eyes showing curiosity. "He's busy at the moment. Is there something I can help you with?"

He motioned to the two other empty desks near his. "There are only three police officers, aside from the chief. We pretty much all do whatever's needed, from investigations to throwing drunks in the tank. I'm sure I can help."

She tightened her hand around the handle of the leather satchel she'd just retrieved from her car in the parking lot at the end of the street before returning to the station. "I really need to speak to your boss first." When he continued to hesitate, she added, "It's really important. My name is Grace Malone, but he won't recognize that name."

He motioned toward a folding chair beside his desk. "Have a seat. I'll let him know you're here, Ms. Malone."

"Thank you."

He headed to the right door of two closed ones on the other side of the room. Gold lettering similar to outside listed the chief's name. A second door bore the traditional male/female restroom symbols. And past that were snack and drink machines and a little table with a coffee maker and supplies. This was definitely a no-frills police station.

After Ortiz headed into the chief's office, another officer came in through the front door carrying a large brown paper bag. The haft of an arrow stuck out from the top with a familiar-looking white feather with a red streak down the middle. He smiled at Grace and glanced around, noting the prisoner in the holding cell who was sitting on a cot watching them. Then he set the bag on top of one of the desks and offered his hand and a friendly smile to Grace.

"Hey, stranger. I'm Officer Chris Collier. May I help you?"

Grace shook his hand. "Grace Malone. Officer Ortiz is letting the chief know that I need to speak to him." She motioned toward the bag. "Is that the arrow that was embedded in the boat at the festival?"

"Sure is. I had to cut a hole in the boat to get it out intact. Bobby was cursing a blue streak the whole time."

"Bobby? The boat owner I presume?"

"Bobby Thompson, owner of the boat and the marina outside of town. He didn't care that it's evidence. Can't say as I blame him for being angry, but there was already a hole from the arrow. He'd have had to make a repair either way. He'll get over his mad once he figures that out. You want something to drink or a snack? We have vending machines, nothing fancy. Everything's free, no charge."

"No, thanks. I'm good for now. I don't mean to take up your time. Go ahead and do whatever you need to do while I wait."

"Not a lot to do around here right now aside from a few petty theft investigations we're working. The festival is prematurely over and everyone's either gone home or to the main restaurant and bar to drown their disappointment." He frowned toward the holding cell. "Thanks to you, O'Brien. What were you thinking letting loose with that arrow so close to people? You could have hurt someone."

In answer, the prisoner crossed his arms. He might not be talking, but he was clearly paying attention to their conversation.

Collier shook his head. "Dang hermit. No telling what was going through his head."

"Hermit?" The word evoked an image of an old man with a long beard and torn, dirty clothes in Grace's mind. The gorgeous well-groomed man behind bars was nothing like that. His neatly trimmed barely-there beard and mustache were complemented by the slightly shaggy hair.

If she were to describe him she'd label him a sexy rebel. Not that it mattered. If he was the one responsible for the shooting today, or turned out to be a serial killer, she'd do everything in her power to bring him to justice.

Collier continued. "He keeps to himself up on the mountain and—"

"Officer Collier, don't you have a report to type and evidence to log?" The police chief stepped out of his office with Ortiz following behind him.

Collier seemed unfazed by his boss's criticism. "Yes, sir. I'll take care of it right away." He picked up the brown bag and carried it toward a line of metal cabinets along the back wall, to the left of the glass-enclosed conference room.

The chief stopped in front of Grace as Ortiz took a seat at his desk. "Ms. Malone, I'm Police Chief Beau Dawson. How can I help you?"

She stood and shook his hand. "Special Agent Grace Malone."

His eyes widened in surprise. "FBI? Homeland Security? ATF?"

"FBI." She showed him her badge, then hefted her satchel. "I need to speak to you. In private."

"We can use my office."

"Actually, unless your office is really large, the table in that conference room might work better. I have a lot of papers and photographs to spread out."

"All right. Ortiz, Mr. O'Brien's parole officer is on her way. When Mrs. Whang arrives, let her speak to her client about what happened at the festival before I interview him."

"Will do, Chief."

As soon as the conference room door closed behind them, Grace set the satchel on the table and faced Dawson. "Your prisoner is on parole? What did he do that landed him in prison?"

Instead of answering her, he asked a question. "Why did the FBI send an agent to Mystic Lake? And why is this the first I'm hearing about it?"

The displeasure in his voice was nothing she hadn't heard dozens of times before from other police or sheriffs. Jurisdiction or just a general distrust of Feds who might try to take over or take the glory for some operation was a real obstacle in her line of work. And as always, she did her best to tamp down her own irritation at once again having to soothe someone's ruffled feathers.

"I'm from the FBI field office in Knoxville. An anonymous tip sent me here to see whether the man I'm looking for might be in Mystic Lake. I did come to the police station first to introduce myself and bring you up to speed. But the station was locked."

His mouth tightened. "Sorry about that. Small town, small police force. When there's a festival, like today, we're spread pretty thin. This anonymous tip you got, what did they tell you?"

"That the killer I'm investigating might be here, that someone who lives in the mountains above town has a bow and arrow and keeps to themselves."

"That's the tip that sent you all the way here from Knoxville?"

"Pretty much. We can't risk ignoring a tip, however weak. You never know which one will pan out. Or which unexplored lead a defense attorney will use to try to drive holes through a future case."

He let out a deep sigh. "I wouldn't put much credence in what they said. You might have noticed the stores up and down the street outside, Main Street, are small boutique shops offering clothes, jewelry, local-made items that are more for the tourists than the town residents. We do have one convenience store of a sort, a locally run place with essentials, perishable goods, medical supplies. But for anything more than that you have to drive at least an hour out of town. That's why most of the people here own rifles or handguns. And for bow hunting season, a surprising number have bows and arrows. Hunting isn't just for sport in Mystic Lake, it's a way to feed our families. Someone telling you to check out a person with a bow and arrow around here is wasting your time." He cocked his head, studying her. "But you don't seem surprised by anything I just said. You knew all of that, didn't you?"

She smiled. "I know what I researched on the internet about this town. I don't pretend to be an expert and I'm sure what I read is likely half the truth, if that. But, yes, I knew most of the inhabitants hunted and likely quite a lot have bows and arrows. But I'm searching for someone who uses something a bit more sophisticated, the kind of bow not allowed for hunting in many places. A crossbow. I'm searching for the Crossbow Killer."

He swore and slowly sat in one of the chairs, a look of dread on his face. "The serial killer I've heard about on the news. He's killed, what, six people so far?"

"That we know of. Yes, sir."

"You think he's here?"

She sat across from him and pulled her satchel toward her. "That anonymous tip was light on details. There's no proof he's operating here or fled here when the heat got bad in Knoxville. But, as I said, we have to follow up on every lead. If it's accurate, and we don't perform our due diligence, people could die."

"And the Feds would be eviscerated in the press, giving the FBI a black eye."

"True. But we're people, too. While we don't want our reputation smeared, it's more important to us that we save lives."

He smiled for the first time since she'd met him. "Touché. All right, I'll answer your original question. The reason that Aidan O'Brien is on parole is because he was convicted of murder. He served ten years in prison and was paroled a little over a year ago. He's not from around here. He's from the Nashville area. From what his parole officer has told me, he petitioned the parole board to allow him to move here. He wanted a fresh start, somewhere that the people might not have heard about his case."

She glanced past him at the man they were discussing. He was still sitting on the cot in his cell. When his dark gaze met hers, he didn't turn away or try to pretend he wasn't watching the chief and her. She vaguely wondered whether or not he could read lips.

"Mr. O'Brien seems keenly interested in our discussion."

Dawson didn't bother to turn around to look. "No doubt. Strangers make him nervous. When the tourists arrive to see the leaves turning or to enjoy our lake in the summer, O'Brien disappears. He's not exactly the outgoing type."

"Understandable. It's hard for a convicted felon to get past people's expectations and fears that he might reoffend. I noted he made a point of avoiding you in particular at the festival."

"Can't blame him. When he first arrived in town and his parole officer briefed me, I put a notice on our internal town website to alert people that a convicted murderer was now among us. It wasn't fair to him to do that. But my priority is to keep my citizens safe. Keeping them informed of potential danger is part of that."

"It's not my place to judge you."

He smiled again. "But you are. I can see it in your eyes. You're young, what, mid-thirties?" He held up a hand to stop her from responding. "Forget I asked. My point is I have a few more years on you and I'm probably a whole lot more jaded. I've learned that people don't typically change. Offenders usually reoffend. Period. So I keep my guard up."

"You expect him to murder again?"

"If you're asking whether he's done anything alarming before today, or showed a propensity toward violence, the answer is no. But I'm open to the possibility and vigilant. I can well imagine you're interested in looking into him, too, given his past, and this morning's incident. You think he could be the killer you're after?"

"I guess I'm like you, open to possibilities. Particularly after I got a quick look at the bow and arrows your people found, and the one that was cut out of the boat. While we don't have any eyewitnesses about the crossbow that our killer uses and what it looks like, we do have confirmation that the kinds of arrows used are made specifically for a crossbow. And the feather with paint down it attached to each arrow is well documented from our crime scenes."

She emptied the contents of the satchel onto the table and fanned through them until she found one particular picture, one that showed the feather that was this particular killer's signature.

He stared down at it a long moment, then turned to

glance at his prisoner before meeting her gaze again. "You have my attention, Special Agent Malone. Show me everything you have and tell me exactly what that anonymous tipster told you."

Chapter Three

Aidan paced the length of the holding cell, which took him all of three strides. He occasionally glanced at the glass-walled room where the chief and the FBI agent had been talking for the past half hour.

He had no clue what they were discussing, but it must be important since the chief was delaying interviewing him. Dawson had flat out told him he believed he was behind that stupid stunt at the festival. Refusing to listen to Aidan's protests, the chief had promised to get the truth out of him after he made a few phone calls to try to calm the town leaders about the ruined festival.

It shouldn't bother Aidan at this point that he was the first person the police picked up whenever something bad happened around here. After all, he was the only parolee in Mystic Lake and this wasn't the first, second or even dozenth time they'd brought him in for questioning. But it *did* bother him. It bothered him more than any of those other times, because this wasn't for something juvenile like knocking over someone's mailbox. This was shooting an arrow into a crowd, something Aidan would never do, especially with innocent children running around. But Chief

Dawson couldn't look beyond Aidan's past. To Dawson, a killer was a killer, regardless of the circumstances.

Aidan stopped pacing and plopped down onto the cot. As always, when he was at the police station he couldn't help thinking about the past. He'd had a family once—a young son he adored, a wife he'd loved so much it hurt. They'd planned to grow old together, to spend their golden years with a score of grandchildren running around their front yard. But that was never going to happen. Not anymore.

He shoved to his feet again to continue pacing.

The front door opened. When Aidan saw who was coming into the station, he groaned. His parole officer was here. His shoulders slumped as he stepped to the bars to greet Mrs. Whang. But instead of taking her to see her client, Collier ushered her into the conference room.

His parole officer was speaking to an FBI agent, presumably about him. This couldn't be good. Visions of having his parole rescinded and being sent back to prison had him sweating. He fisted his hands at his sides and waited at the cell door to be taken to the chief's office, where he and his parole officer always met in private.

She wasn't in the conference room for long. But whatever they'd told her had a notable impact. Her face was pale and drawn as she headed toward him. But rather than one of the officers letting him out to speak with her, Whang stood outside the locked door to his cell.

"Mr. O'Brien. We need to talk."

A few minutes later, Whang left and it was Aidan's turn to be led to the conference room. For the first time since leaving prison, in addition to handcuffs he was wearing leg shackles. He clenched his jaw against the added humiliation of two officers, Collier and Ortiz, escorting him into the conference room. Even more humiliating was what his parole officer had told him.

That he was under suspicion of being a serial killer.

Maybe it was a good thing that he was cuffed and shackled. Because right now a burning rage was flowing through his veins like molten lava. If his hands had been free he'd have likely punched a hole through a wall, or slammed a chair against one of the glass walls of the conference room.

Ortiz motioned Aidan to sit at the far end of the table. Once Aidan was seated, the officer secured the length of chain between his handcuffs to the steel ring bolted into the top of the table. Collier did the same with the leg shackle chain underneath the table, attaching it to a steel ring on the floor that Aidan had never even noticed before. No doubt he had the FBI agent to thank for being trussed up and for blackening his reputation even more than it already had been.

As the door closed, the agent smiled and nodded, since hand-shaking was obviously out of the question. Aidan wouldn't have shaken her hand anyway. Right now he considered her enemy number one, ruining what little progress he'd made over the past year. Gossip blew through this town like the winds coming down off the mountains. By the time he was released—if he was released—everyone in Mystic Lake would be talking about his past again, and speculating about whether he was this so-called Crossbow Killer.

"Mr. O'Brien, I'm Special Agent Grace Malone. I work out of the FBI field office in Knoxville. If you don't mind, I'd like to ask you a few questions."

He sat back, grateful that the handcuff chain was long enough to allow him that small comfort.

"I do mind. I'm already under arrest for allegedly shooting an arrow through a crowd of people, an arrow that could have killed children, let alone the two adults on that boat. If you're here to arrest me for something I haven't done, get in line." He rattled the chains hanging from his handcuffs.

Her eyes widened.

Dawson swore. "We caught you with your bow and arrows after you ran into the woods to get away."

Aidan leaned forward in his chair, desperately trying to tamp down his anger. But it was impossible to completely hide that he was mad as hell.

"Let's deal in facts instead of conjecture, Chief. Fact— you found a bow and a quiver of arrows lying in the woods about ten yards behind where I'd been sitting on the hill, watching the festival. Fact—you don't know yet whose they are. We both agree that they likely belong to whoever shot that arrow. Officer Collier's your resident fingerprint expert, isn't he? Have him compare any prints on the weapon to my prints that you have on file. I guarantee they won't match."

Malone held up her hands. "Hold it. Let's step back a minute. First of all, Chief Dawson, I'd very much like to have your permission to send the evidence from the festival to the FBI lab for forensic examination. They can test for DNA on some parts and fingerprints on others. If that's done in the wrong order it can ruin our chances to get a profile or viable prints."

"How quickly can the FBI get that done?"

"The Crossbow Killer case is one of our highest priorities right now. I can have a courier pick it up this afternoon and have results in a few days."

"That's far better than me sending it to our state lab, which can take months. Keep me informed on the results.

We'll get everything ready for transport. It'll be ready for your courier."

"Thank you."

Aidan wanted to shout his frustration about any kind of delay in proving his innocence. But he knew that wouldn't do any good, so he remained silent.

"Mr. O'Brien," the agent said. "The second thing I wanted to do was ask you, if you really aren't the shooter, why did you run away when Chief Dawson took off after you?"

"Lady, I didn't even know Dawson was there until he tackled me from behind. I wasn't running *from* anyone. I was running *after* someone, the idiot who sent an arrow whizzing past my ear."

Dawson's jaw tightened with anger. "You expect us to believe that the only person in town who's an admitted, confessed killer—you—just happened to be sitting where another killer, or would-be killer, takes a potshot from the woods? And then that phantom guy happens to drop his weapon as he runs away, making it look as if you're the shooter? Is that the cockamamie story you're trying to feed us?"

Aidan's voice was hoarse from suppressing the urge to shout as he responded. "What I want you to believe is the truth. I don't have all the answers. Conducting an investigation isn't my job. It's yours. But if you want to pin this on me, I'm warning you right now. I won't go down without a fight. I'm not pleading guilty to make your job easier."

Malone held her hands up again in a placating gesture. "I don't believe anyone here is trying to pin anything on you. Chief Dawson and I are both after the same thing as you—the truth. Let's try to set aside hurt feelings or even theories and focus on the facts, just as you suggested. You said someone behind you shot over your shoulder. When you turned around, were you able to get a look at them? Do you think you can give us a description?"

Dawson crossed his arms. "*I* can. The shooter is male, white, six-foot-two, late thirties with brown eyes, shaggy brown hair and light facial hair wearing a dark T-shirt, jean jacket, jeans and brown hiking boots."

The exact description of Aidan had him trying to jump to his feet but the shackles forced him down into the chair without being able to stand upright. He glared his outrage. But before he could respond, Malone rapped her knuckles on the table to get their attention.

Her blue eyes flashed with anger of her own as she looked at Dawson. "That didn't help things one bit, Chief. Unless you actually saw the shooter and he was Mr. O'Brien's twin."

Dawson's face reddened slightly. "I couldn't swear in court who shot the arrow. But it's obvious who did."

Malone rolled her eyes. "We'll have fingerprint and DNA analysis in a few days. That should help all of us."

Dawson stood. "I'll get my team working on readying the evidence for your lab."

As soon as the door closed behind the chief, Malone blew out a deep breath. "Okay. Let's try this again. Mr. O'Brien, if you're truly innocent, I well understand your frustration and anger. But I assure you that making assumptions and going down the wrong path in my investigation is the absolute last thing I want. If I pursue the wrong person, the real killer is free to continue his sick games. More people will die. That's not something I want on my conscience. You may not believe me, but we both want the same thing. The truth."

He'd only just met her. He didn't know anything about her other than her name and occupation. And yet her blue eyes were unflinching, clear, looking at him the way an honest person might, with seemingly nothing to hide. Her petite frame was relaxed. Her pink lips weren't tightened with indignation or disgust as some people's were when around him, knowing he was a convicted felon. The tailored navy blue blazer she wore, the perfect straight brown hair pulled back into a ponytail, screamed integrity to him. She was the quintessential federal agent. But she was still young enough to be somewhat inexperienced, idealistic, and naively believe that truth and justice were the same thing.

He knew better.

The truth could ruin lives, destroy people, annihilate families. Sometimes a lie was the only way to save someone. But that was a lesson he hoped this bright young woman never had to learn. He hoped she could cling to her idealism and view of justice forever and never experience the bitterness he tasted every single day.

"You want the truth?" he asked.

"Yes. Please."

He relaxed back in his chair. "All right. The truth. As a convicted felon, I'm not allowed to own a gun or even a hunting knife. The knives in my kitchen are dull butter knives. If I want to cut a steak, I have to use a pair of meat scissors like they use in Korea to cut their meat. When I take down a deer, a rabbit, a turkey, I can't clean and carve it for my own use even though I know how. I have to take them all the way to Chattanooga to have a chop house process them and package them for my freezer. That's a price I pay for the crime to which I pleaded guilty, and I accept that. I only bring it up because in spite of those restrictions, I *am* allowed a bow and arrows. I had to petition the court for special permission so I could use them to hunt, only on my own property, and for self-defense in case a bear ever comes after me. It took months, but my request was approved. I've become an expert with a bow, which is one of the reasons the chief is so willing to believe that I'm guilty of what happened today."

"But you're not?"

"No, Special Agent Malone. I'm not. Can I prove I didn't shoot today? No. But the question that really matters is can you, or Dawson, prove that I did? Unless one of you falsifies evidence, the answer is no. I've killed once in my life, over twelve years ago now. I went to prison, served my time, paid the price that society placed on my crime. It's over, done, in my past, and that's where I'd like it to stay. I'm not the serial killer you came here searching for. Now it's your turn. Truth. Why are you even looking at me for the murders you're trying to solve? Why did you come to Mystic Lake?"

She gave him a lopsided smile. "Fate maybe. If what you've said is accurate, if you have nothing to do with the murders I'm investigating, then maybe you can end up helping me instead of being a suspect. I could use an expert on bows and arrows. It sounds like you might be one."

"Somehow I can't quite see the FBI not having some obscure expert on staff who can answer any questions you have about that type of weapon."

"Humor me."

He hesitated. "What do you want to know?"

"The arrows that were found today, couldn't they be shot with a regular bow, not just with a crossbow?"

"Not likely. Arrows for a crossbow are shorter. Some call

them bolts, rather than arrows. They're not interchangeable with the kind I use, for a regular bow. They're not even interchangeable with a compound bow."

"Compound bow?"

"It's something barely resembling a traditional bow. It has gears and pulleys and a lot of plastic. Not to my taste. If the arrows you've found at crime scenes are less than, say, twenty-two inches, they come from a crossbow. The kind I use are around thirty inches. But I'm guessing you knew that already. That's basic information to have researched when looking for a killer using a bow."

"You're right, to an extent. I knew the experts concluded the killer's using a crossbow because of the size of the arrow. But I wanted to make sure there wasn't some kind of exception, that their conclusions are correct. Like maybe a particular bow is supposed to use a different length arrow, but the killer is using another kind to throw us off."

"Not likely. Using the wrong length or even weight of arrow can not only destroy accuracy, it can be dangerous. Think of it the way you do guns. Different ammunition is designed for different types of guns. They're not interchangeable. I don't think you're dealing with a bow-and-arrow expert here, though. Even if he did want to throw investigators off in some way, he's not smart enough or experienced enough to know how to do it without hurting himself."

"Why do you say that?"

"The fletching on the arrows that were found today is all wrong."

"Fletching. You're talking about the fins on the end of the arrow."

"You did your homework."

She smiled. "I've read the files. We'll leave it at that. I know the fletching is for aerodynamics. Sometimes it's feathers, sometimes plastic. Our guy uses both."

"Technically, no. He doesn't. The arrows I saw today had—"

The door to the conference room opened and Chief Dawson stepped inside, holding a thick manila folder. Behind him was Officer Ortiz.

Ortiz headed to the end of the table where Aidan was sitting and knelt on the floor beneath it. The sound of chains falling had Aidan blinking in surprise. A moment later his handcuffs were removed and Ortiz left the room.

Aidan remained seated, rubbing his wrists and testing out the new freedom of movement of his legs, all while suspiciously watching Dawson.

"What's going on?" he asked. "Is this some kind of game?"

"No game. The interview is over. Mr. O'Brien, you're free to go. There will be no charges pressed against you for today's…incident."

Aidan eagerly stood, but his pathway to the door was suddenly blocked by Malone.

"Just a minute," she said. "Chief, even if you're dropping charges, I'd like to speak to Mr. O'Brien about my case. We were just discussing—"

"You can speak to him later," Dawson said. "Mr. O'Brien, I didn't see your truck in the parking lot down the street or anywhere out front. Do you need a ride home?"

"My motorbike's parked a few blocks down."

"Chief Dawson," Grace said. "I really wish you'd wait and—"

"Excuse me." Aidan brushed past her and quickly left.

Once he reached his motorcycle, he hesitated. The man he'd been so long ago seemed to be stirring to life inside him, trying to guilt him into going back to finish answering the questions Malone had. But he viciously tamped down those softer feelings. She didn't need him, not really. She was with the FBI, after all. There were plenty of resources she could use to find out what he'd already figured out.

That this so-called Crossbow Killer wasn't targeting his victims.

They were all random. If law enforcement was focusing their investigation on learning about the victims and looking for links between them, they were wasting their time.

The aerodynamics of that arrow would have been thrown off so much by that long dangling feather that hitting that boat this morning was completely by chance. The shooter was more than likely just letting the arrow fly and didn't care who it hit. Did Special Agent Malone know that? How could she not? Someone in the FBI would have studied those arrows and come to the same conclusions he had and put it in that large file of hers she'd had sitting on the table. Which meant that Malone didn't actually need him.

More than likely, her questions had all been a pretense. She just wanted to keep him talking, hoping he'd get comfortable, slip up and confess to a crime he didn't commit.

His conscience quietened, if not fully assuaged, he put on his helmet and sent his bike roaring down the street.

Chapter Four

Grace caught a brief glimpse of her only potential suspect zipping past the front windows of the police station on his motorcycle. If it was up to her, he'd still be sitting at the end of the conference table answering her questions. Instead, she was reorganizing her documentation and stowing it back in her satchel as the police chief stood on the other side of the table, still holding the folder he'd brought with him when he'd come back into the conference room.

"I'd like an explanation," she said. "You let my suspect go and didn't even have the courtesy to speak to me about it first."

He arched a brow. "You're right. I should have spoken to you first. However, I felt I owed it to Mr. O'Brien to release him immediately." He pulled out his phone and swiped his thumb across the screen before handing it to her.

She stared at the picture, stunned. "Where did you get this?"

"I had another one of my officers, Fletcher, canvassing the people at the festival who were near the hill when the arrow was shot. When I was telling Collier to package up the evidence for the FBI lab, I called Fletcher to see how her canvassing was going. She told me that one of the families she'd spoken to had been taking pictures on that hill not too far from where O'Brien was sitting. They texted her that picture you're looking at."

"They caught the arrow in flight, going right past O'Brien's shoulder."

Dawson nodded. "Unfortunately, the person who shot that arrow is in the shadows of the trees and can't be seen. But this is proof positive that O'Brien isn't the shooter at the festival."

She handed him back the phone. "Agreed. He's not today's shooter. But that doesn't mean he's not the Crossbow Killer. He uses bows and arrows to hunt. And he's a convicted murderer in a town where an anonymous tipster said I'd find my killer. I wouldn't be doing my job if I didn't look deeper to either rule him out in my investigation, or keep him on my list."

"You have a list of suspects?"

"Officially, no. But we have a handful of persons of interest other agents are checking out in other locations. For now, I'm only looking at Mystic Lake. And O'Brien's my only suspect at this point. But after that festival incident, and seeing those white feathers with a red line painted down the center, it sure looks like either my killer is here, or there's a copycat. He's either just as deadly, or someone having fun, playing with the police."

Dawson groaned. "I sure hope we don't have a copycat. Someone toying with us though, that wouldn't really surprise me. Some of the teenagers around here like to have fun adding to the town's reputation for unusual or unexplained events. I can just see one of them doing this, not really trying to hurt anyone, but trying to cause a stir around town. I'll start looking into the usual culprits, see what I can find out."

"Tourism is the main industry here, isn't it?" she asked.

"During summer and fall, yes. Leaf peepers and those wanting to boat or kayak or even camp near the larger part of the lake outside of town. But most of the people around here either commute to a job in Chattanooga every day or work remotely online. Why?"

"I'm wondering about your local economy. A lot of places that rely heavily on tourism have suffered from things like the pandemic and ups and downs in the economy since then. Could someone other than the teens you mentioned be trying to put the town more on the map, generate media and tourist interest by making it look like the Crossbow Killer is operating here?"

He grimaced. "I prefer the juvenile delinquent angle than to think an adult would be that reckless. But, point taken. We'll explore every possibility, not just focusing on our problem kids around here. As for you talking more to O'Brien, I can place another call to his parole officer to have her arrange another chat. He doesn't really have a choice, given the conditions of his parole. However, I've found that the more background I have on a suspect, the more prepared I am to get something worthwhile out of an interrogation. That's another reason I let him go earlier. I wanted you to be able to read through this first."

He finally set down the folder he'd been holding.

"What is it?" she asked as she slid her last stack of pictures into her satchel.

"Aidan O'Brien's arrest record and background on the crime for which he was convicted. It's a copy of the folder his parole officer gave me when O'Brien relocated here.

I'm sure you can get the full investigative file if you want it. I never had a reason to dig deeper and request more information."

After quickly flipping through the contents, she frowned. "I don't see a trial transcript."

"There wasn't a trial. He pled guilty."

"What about his sentencing hearing?"

"Like I said, I didn't dig deeper. You'll have to make a records request if you want a transcript of that. Collier made that folder for you. You can keep it."

"Thanks. I appreciate it." She slid it into her satchel and strapped it over her shoulder. "I'll call my office from my car, arrange for a courier to pick up your evidence. Shouldn't take more than a few hours to get someone here."

"We'll be ready." He held the conference room door open for her.

At the front door, she stopped. "One more thing. If the evidence is authenticated, if the Bureau confirms it's consistent with the evidence we already have, be prepared for a few more agents heading this way to help with my investigation."

"Trust me," he said, "if there's a serial killer in my town, I'm grateful for any help you can provide. There won't be any jurisdictional fights or egos getting in the way. We'll take this guy down, together, whoever he is."

She smiled. "That's wonderful to hear. It will make everything easier, and faster."

He handed her a business card. "My office and mobile are on there. When you're ready to set up another meeting with O'Brien, just shout." He pointed toward a two-story whitewashed cottage on the other side of the lake. "That's Stella's Bed and Breakfast. Locals use it to house family and friends that come to visit. And once tourists start bombarding us in a few weeks, the place fills up fast. But there are probably a few vacancies right now. Stella's main source of income is actually the restaurant downstairs. It's open seven days a week and is the best place in town for a hot meal. I highly recommend it."

She smiled her thanks. "I'll head there now and see if you're right about vacancies. I'd assumed I'd have to stay in Chattanooga and drive in each day that I'm here. Stella's would be much more convenient."

After shaking his hand, she headed down the brick sidewalk toward the parking lot at the end of Main Street. Although the only parking she saw on the other side of the lake was parallel street parking, she couldn't imagine the B and B and its large, attached restaurant not having parking for the customers. There must be a lot behind it or maybe farther down the street on that side of the lake. She figured she'd head over there and find out. If she was wrong, she'd just park back at the large lot at the end of Main Street and walk around the lake to Stella's.

As she'd hoped, there was indeed a good-sized lot behind the B and B. She just had to go a block down and loop back behind the row of shops to get to it. The bumpy gravel and incline that led up to Stella's lot had her grateful she'd insisted on a four-wheel drive vehicle when she'd rented the SUV. It would be handy when she checked out the marina and campground she'd researched, too. Both were about a mile out of town where the lake widened and deepened and attracted boaters and fisherman. There were even some class two and three rapids where the river flowed down from the mountains and fed the lake.

Having learned to pack light over the years, all she had

to bring inside the B and B was a small rolling suitcase and her satchel that contained her laptop, her investigative files and notes. The check-in desk downstairs doubled both for the inn and the surprisingly busy restaurant. It seemed that half the town must be either at the bar or sitting at the tables and booths drinking or eating. No doubt with the festival canceled, they were finding another way to have the fun they'd been denied.

The owner herself, Stella Holman, checked Grace in, reserving a room for her plus two more at Grace's request in case more agents were needed in the next few days. After Stella took Grace upstairs to her room and was about to head downstairs again, Grace stopped her.

"Ms. Holman?"

The petite, white-haired lady smiled. "It's Mrs., but we don't stand on formality around here. Call me Stella. How can I help you, dear?"

"I need to go see someone up in the mountains a little later. I have the address, but it's not showing up on my GPS."

Stella laughed. "If you go by those fancy GPS things around here you'll get lost every time, or drive off a cliff. Half the time phones don't even work in these mountains. What's the address?"

"It's on Niall's Circle."

The other woman's smile faltered. "I see. Well, that won't be on your GPS because it's not the official name of any road. It's basically a driveway. A very long one, but technically a driveway. Head out of town and take the first right up Harper Road. You'll find the turnoff to Niall's Circle at the top of the mountain, where Harper ends. I can draw it out if you need me to."

"No, no. Those directions sound easy to follow. Thanks so much."

Stella patted Grace's shoulder. "I hope you enjoy our little town, maybe take a boat out on the lake. It's gorgeous this time of year. If you're hungry, come downstairs for lunch before you go sightseeing. With the festival canceled, there's a party going on. There's a game room, too, with tables set up for cards, some pool tables and even a dartboard. I'm sure you'd have fun. And the food's not bad either. I hear that Mr. Holman is an excellent chef." She winked and headed downstairs.

Grace briefly debated going downstairs right now. Not to party or eat, but to mingle with the townspeople to try to get information that might help her investigation. But as loud as it had been when she'd passed the opening to the restaurant before coming upstairs, it was doubtful that conversations would be easy or fruitful. She'd have to make the rounds another time.

Talking to O'Brien was her number one priority anyway. And she had no intention of notifying his parole officer or having him return to the station at this point. Instead, she wanted to surprise him, catch him off guard at his own home, on Niall's Circle. If he was comfortable, in his own element, it would be easier to build that rapport she'd need to get him to speak freely.

She put her things away, then sat down on the king-size bed she'd splurged the FBI's money on and made a call to the office. Her favorite admin took down the information that Grace gave her, promising to email her the full investigative file on O'Brien, including a transcript of the sentencing hearing along with one from the parole hearing if she could get that released. Sometimes those weren't shared. Well, most of the time they weren't. But when the FBI asked for something, they usually got it. And this particular admin was a bulldog when it came to getting what the agents needed. If anyone could get it, she could.

Her next call was to her boss, Supervisory Special Agent Levi Perry. He wasn't happy that she'd driven the three hours here and spent several more hours in town before checking in without calling. He was a stickler for knowing where his agents were at all times. Not because he was controlling or a micromanager, but because safety was his number one concern. Grace suffered through the usual lecture about being careful and checking in daily. Then she gave him an update on everything that had happened since her arrival, as well as her plan to interview O'Brien as soon as she read up on his background.

"Just follow all protocols and be on your guard the whole time," he warned. "It doesn't sound like this is our guy, given that someone else shot that arrow. But with his background, he could still be dangerous. And while I agree you're more likely to get him to let his guard down and speak freely at his place, if any red flags go up while you're there, end the interview immediately and have his parole officer order him to the police station for further questioning."

"Of course. Absolutely. I'll be careful."

"I know you will or I wouldn't have sent you there on your own."

"You wouldn't have sent me here at all if you thought there was really a chance our killer was here. But I still appreciate you finally cutting the strings and letting me do some investigating without a supervisor watching my every move."

"Don't thank me too soon. If the lab determines the

arrows you have on the way are consistent and the paint matches the arrows we already have in evidence, you won't be on your own anymore. That's not a statement about your readiness to be a full-fledged agent. It's a statement about how dangerous this killer is that we're after. I don't want to add one of my agents to his victim list."

"Understood. I'll keep you posted. And if the lab confirms our killer is here, I'll stand down immediately and wait for backup to continue the investigation."

"Regardless of what the lab determines, use all those skills you've been practicing under Special Agent Kingsley's mentorship. Approach every assignment as if it's the most important, and potentially dangerous one you've ever worked and you'll always come out ahead. Got it?"

"Yes, sir."

"Keep me updated."

The call ended and Grace blew out a relieved breath. Someone on the outside looking in would think her boss was being extremely protective because she was a woman. But she knew better. He was this way with all his agents, particularly the ones like her who were finally out of training and no longer working under the guidance of another agent. While she appreciated that he wanted everyone working for him to be safe, it could be smothering at times.

Her final call was to the lab to make sure they had no questions about what needed to be done once the evidence arrived. They assured her they'd log it in and assign a technician to it immediately. Even so, unless the fingerprints were found to be a match to someone in the Bureau's Integrated Automated Fingerprint Identification System, IAFIS, then it would likely take several more days to get results on any DNA.

If the person who'd shot that arrow had been arrested for a felony in the past and the arresting agency had entered their DNA profile into the Combined DNA Index System, then CODIS would spit out the name of a potential suspect. A hit on either IAFIS or CODIS could make their investigation take off. But not if the arrows from Mystic Lake didn't match the arrows already known to have come from the Crossbow Killer.

The absence of viable prints or DNA on the evidence was another very real possibility. Which meant she needed to stop counting on the lab's potential results and start pounding the pavement to determine if the anonymous tip was right or not.

Her boss agreed with her decision to interview O'Brien even though he wasn't the one who'd shot that arrow today. Because yet another theory they'd discussed was that if O'Brien was the actual Crossbow Killer, he could have realized someone suspected him and that they may have called in a tip. The best way to throw law enforcement off his trail would be to hire someone else to shoot that arrow during the festival where there'd be lots of witnesses. And having someone take a picture just as the arrow was being shot over O'Brien's shoulder, well, that was either incredible luck or a well thought out plan. The person who took the picture could have been paid, too. She'd have to contact the police and get the name of the person who took the picture so she could interview them, as well.

But first, she needed to focus on O'Brien.

The biggest question in her mind right now was the identity of his victim all those years ago and the alleged motive behind the murder. Dawson hadn't volunteered that information. And she'd planned on asking O'Brien about it at the station after first building some rapport with him. With the interview ending so unexpectedly, she'd never gotten the chance.

Even knowing that the man was a murderer, it was hard to believe. He was well-spoken, sounded well-educated, and money didn't seem to be a problem for him to solve by killing someone for their assets. The motorcycle he'd ridden wasn't exactly cheap. The chief had mentioned that O'Brien owned a truck, too. And O'Brien himself had talked about hunting on his own land. It didn't sound as if he was hurting financially, so a financial motive seemed unlikely.

Other common motives for murder were love and revenge. Did one of those explain why he'd crossed that terrible line and taken the life of someone else years ago? Or was he a thrill killer, a sociopath who took the lives of people as a way of playing God and experiencing the high of total control over another person's life?

Three pages into O'Brien's folder, the identity of who he'd killed had her frozen in shock. The man she'd met couldn't have done that, could he? But there it was in black-and-white as she read it again. The woman he'd murdered all those years ago was Elly O'Brien. His wife.

Chapter Five

Aidan crossed his arms and leaned against the railing of the front steps of his cabin, watching the black SUV coming down the long driveway through his property. It was straight, by design. It gave him plenty of time to see anyone coming. And to prepare to either welcome them, which was rare and reserved for only a few, or turn them away. Since none of his extremely small group of friends drove a vehicle like that, turning them away was exactly what he planned to do.

But when the driver's door opened and Special Agent Grace Malone emerged from the vehicle, he swore beneath his breath. If she had been a civilian, ordering her off his property was a given. He had every right, even as a felon, to make her leave. But an FBI agent? Since he was on parole, he was at her mercy. He couldn't make her do one damn thing. Unless she allowed it.

As she approached, he forced himself to ignore the way his breath hitched at seeing her curvy little body again, or the way he was instantly intrigued by the intelligence shining out of those incredibly blue eyes. It didn't matter that her smile made his gut tighten with desire. She wasn't his friend or a potential lover.

She was his enemy.

He needed to remember that. She was a Trojan horse, compelling and beautiful on the outside but deadly on the inside. The only reason he was this affected by her had to be because he wasn't used to being close to a beautiful woman these days. So few women dared to get anywhere near him. His unwelcome reaction to the agent certainly wasn't because there was something special about her. And it wouldn't matter if there was. She worked for the FBI. That alone was reason to avoid her.

Her smile broadened as she stopped in front of him and held out her hand. "Mr. O'Brien, it's good to see you again. Grace Malone, in case you've forgotten since this morning."

He glanced at her hand, but didn't take it. "I haven't forgotten, Special Agent Malone. You're trespassing. Leave."

She dropped her hand, her smile still firmly in place. "Irish, right? That slight brogue. It's barely noticeable, but it's there. Your family is from Ireland?"

"I'm busy, working. I've got nothing to say to you, so return to your vehicle and head back down the mountain."

She sighed as if arguing with a recalcitrant child. "We both know the conditions of your parole. We can either talk here or I can escort you to the police station. Your choice."

He stepped toward her until they were only a few feet apart, forcing her to crane her neck back to meet his gaze. To her credit, she didn't move or cower away. If she was intimidated by his size or his reputation, she was doing an admirable job of hiding it.

"Special Agent Malone—"

"Call me Grace. I'll call you Aidan."

"Special Agent Malone, I'm a convicted murderer. You're standing at the top of a mountain, alone, with me. The nearest neighbor is halfway down this mountain and likely not even home this time of day. You could scream as loud as you want and no one would hear it. You being here must mean that you still think I could be this serial killer you're looking for. Think very carefully. Are you really sure you want to play your law enforcement trump card to stick around and try to force me to answer your questions? Without backup?"

She flipped back her jacket, revealing a shoulder holster and the butt of a pistol sticking out of it. "This is my backup."

He snorted with reluctant amusement. "You're gutsy. I'll give you that. I'll also give you a tip. Standing this close to me, it doesn't matter that you have a gun. I could wrestle you to the ground or snap your neck before you'd have a chance to draw."

Her smile disappeared and she quickly moved out of his reach. "Is that what you want to do, Aidan? Snap my neck?"

"It's Mr. O'Brien to you. And if I wanted to snap your neck, you'd already be dead. I'm giving free advice I learned the hard way, after spending a decade in prison. I've seen the horrible things that human beings can do to each other, things I never thought I'd see. And I pray to God you never do, even if you are in law enforcement."

"What do you have against law enforcement? No one framed you. You didn't even go to trial because you confessed, pled guilty. You weren't mistreated by the justice system."

"If you consider the time before I went to prison, I agree with you. I got a fair shake. It's once they lock you up that everything changes. Ever wonder why recidivism is so high, why convicted felons reoffend at such a phenomenal rate after getting out of prison? It's because the guards, law enforcement, everyone in the justice system treats them like animals while they're locked up. Security for those in prison is a joke. There isn't any. You have to be vigilant all the time, learn to be a light sleeper, watch your back constantly. I despise everything about the system from beginning to end because there's no humanity or mercy in it. I'm wary of police, of people like you, because one wrong step and I can be snatched from my home and thrown back behind bars. I may look as if I'm free, but it's in name only. I have to watch my back all the time or my life can change in a blink. Good people can go to prison, Malone, because they make some kind of terrible mistake. But whether you were good or not going in, you're a completely changed person coming out."

She stared at him, eyes wide. "Is that what you think? That you were a good person going in? Does a good person murder their wife?"

He could feel his face flushing with heat as anger rode him hard.

She subtly moved her jacket, giving her better access to her weapon if she needed it.

He swore and turned around, heading toward his workshop building on the far side of the cabin. At first, he thought maybe she'd changed her mind about risking being around him, that she was heading to her car. Unfortunately, a moment later he heard her footsteps behind him. From the sound of it, she was keeping well back, not so close he could turn around and grab her. At least his safety lecture had gotten through to her. Who knows? Maybe his advice would save her life in the future when dealing with some other criminal.

Not that he should care—about her, about anyone these

days. He tried not to, especially when people treated him like the man they believed him to be. The townspeople often went out of their way to avoid him, making it painfully obvious they were afraid of him or that they despised him for his past. Perhaps because he understood how they felt, and knew he'd likely feel the same in their position, he couldn't hate them for it or even hold it against them.

But he wished it didn't bother him so much.

And he wished he could ignore when he saw someone in trouble. Like at the festival when that arrow flew past him and into the boat. He was so angry that someone had shot close to children that he'd whirled around and run after the shooter without once thinking about what might happen to him.

And it hadn't done one whit of good.

The police had thrown him into a cell and immediately branded him the villain while the real villain got away. Even now he wasn't sure why the chief had dropped the charges. Maybe because Dawson was stepping back to let the FBI agent have first dibs at him, convinced he was the serial killer she was after.

Rounding the end of the cabin, he stepped through the enormous double doors that were standing open on his workshop. Stopping beside the table in the middle of the building, he picked up the sander he'd been about to use before he heard an engine coming down his driveway.

"Whoa, are you making that?" she asked.

He was careful to set the sander on the table before turning, not wanting to do anything that might seem threatening and could end with a bullet in his chest. But Malone wasn't even looking at him. She was staring at the table, her eyes wide.

She stepped forward almost reverently and gently smoothed her hand across the wood, over the rounded edge. "This is incredible. Your work?"

He nodded, mesmerized by the gentle movement of her hand.

Her fingers continued to slide across the wood as if she couldn't help herself. The pleasure in her expression was such a joy to behold, all he could do was stare.

"Purpleheart wood, right?" She glanced up in question.

He blinked in surprise. "You're familiar with it?"

"I know of it, but have never seen it in person." Her cheeks flushed a dull pink. "I'm pretty sure I saw it on an episode of a house renovation show on TV. But it's so beautiful I didn't forget about it. Is this for your cabin?"

"It's a custom order for a man in Montana, for his deck. He wanted something beautiful for outdoor dining that could withstand the harsh weather without being ruined. Purpleheart wood is extremely hard, resistant to insects, rot, decay."

She sighed and stepped back. "It's gorgeous. Will the color stay that brilliant purple?"

"Not forever, no. But I'll put a UV protectant finish on it that should help it keep its color for several decades." He noted the wistful look on her face as she admired the table again. "Have you ever done carpentry?"

"Only if you count using a block of sandpaper to help my dad in his shop behind our house. Woodworking was one of his many hobbies. He didn't make furniture, certainly nothing grand like you're making. But my mom and I got new handmade jewelry boxes every birthday and he put custom molding all over our house. The shelving in the garage was his pride and joy. I wouldn't say he was an expert or even really good at carpentry, but he enjoyed it."

"Sounds like you enjoyed it, too, or would have, if he'd let you do more than sand."

She smiled. "I didn't want to do anything more difficult than sanding. I didn't crave the experience of hammering or sawing, nothing like that. What I did crave was my father's attention. He always wanted a son and got a daughter instead. Helping him out, even if it was just to fetch tools or sweep sawdust, made him happy. And that made me happy."

"Daddy's little girl."

"Daddy's little tomboy to be more precise. Did you have your little boy with you watching you do woodwork? His name is Niall, right?"

His heart seemed to clench in his chest at her callous reminder about his son. It took him several moments to gather his composure as best he could. "It's getting late. I'll finish this up tomorrow." He began putting his tools up.

Once again she surprised him. She helped him gather his hand saws and chisels and expertly figured out where they went, putting them up on the pegboard wall exactly where they belonged. When she finally faced him, he motioned toward the broom in the corner.

"Are you going to sweep, too?"

"You wish."

He laughed. "I'll do it tomorrow, or later tonight. Come on. The cabin's more comfortable for an interrogation. It's starting to get chilly out here."

"I'm not going to interrogate you."

"Regardless of how you try to soften it, you're here to ask questions. You've brought up my past twice now. And

I know darn well it wasn't my sparkling personality that got you to drive all the way up here."

"Fair enough. I do want to talk. I need to ask some tough questions, too. I hope you'll answer them."

"So you can arrest me?"

"So I can rule you all the way in, or totally out as a suspect if you truly have no bearing on my case."

"At least you're honest." They both stepped outside and he slid the doors shut and settled the wooden bar through the handles to keep wild animals out. He motioned toward the cabin. "Are you okay going inside my cabin? Or do you prefer the porch? Unlike this workshop, there are chairs up there but it will be cold."

She snugged her jacket closer. "I don't want to inconvenience you any more than necessary—"

"Too late for that."

"Are you always this ornery or am I special?"

He cocked his head. "This is me being nice."

She let out a bark of laughter, then cupped her hands over her mouth, obviously mortified that she'd done so.

"Don't worry," he said. "I won't tell your boss that you dared to laugh at a killer."

Her jaw tightened and she dropped her hands. "I wish you wouldn't talk like that. I'm trying to give you the benefit of the doubt. There are things I read in your file that, well, I'd like a better understanding of what happened to put you in prison."

"Why? What's my past got to do with anything you're investigating?"

"Maybe nothing. Maybe everything. You never know what piece of information will be helpful and what won't until you put the whole puzzle together."

"That only makes sense if I'm the one you're calling the Crossbow Killer."

She arched a brow.

He swore. "Fine. We'll talk. But you'll have to brave my lair to do so. I'm no longer willing to be cold on the porch for you."

Without waiting for her, he jogged up the steps to the wraparound porch and headed around to the front door.

Chapter Six

Aidan left the front door open and headed into the kitchen area, having no doubt that Malone would follow him inside the cabin. She was tenacious and wasn't about to leave without getting what she came for. He just hoped that wasn't him, in handcuffs.

"Holy moly," she breathed as she came inside.

He grabbed a bottle of beer and a bottle of water from the refrigerator and carried them to the round table in the front right corner of the cabin. He set the water on the table, opposite him, and twisted open the beer for himself. As Malone toured her way around the great room of the cabin, mouth slightly open in wonder, he sipped his beer and watched her. Part of him couldn't help feeling pride at her wide-eyed surprise as she ran her soft-looking hands over the rocking chairs, end tables, even the wooden animals he'd painstakingly carved over the past year for the grandchildren he'd likely never have.

She headed into the kitchen area just past him and stood in the middle, turning in a slow circle. "The cabinets," she said. "Maple?"

He nodded. "Locally sourced."

"Beautiful. You made those, along with most everything

in the cabin? They have the same look, the same…expert craftsmanship as that table in your workshop."

"They're my work, yes." He took another sip, telling himself not to let his ego get the best of him. Maybe she was impressed with his work, or maybe this was all part of a facade to make him like her, to feel comfortable enough to tell her whatever it was that she wanted to know. She wasn't his friend, wasn't on his side. He needed to remember that, no matter how much a part of him wished it could be different. The one consistent thing about his life ever since his wife's death was an aching loneliness that no amount of hard work could fill, no matter how desperately he tried.

She finally joined him at the table, ignoring the chair across from him and instead sitting beside him. Maybe she hadn't learned that lesson he'd tried to teach her after all, about getting too close to a potentially dangerous person.

"It's incredible, gorgeous," she said. "Everything you've built here. The cabin is amazing, too. These two-story-high ceilings are stunning. The carved banister on the staircase is amazing. And the picture windows frame the mountains like a master painter. Did you build this home, too?"

"Didn't need to. I was lucky enough to find this place already here when I moved to Mystic Lake. The previous owner was retiring to Montana to be with his kids. He's the one who commissioned the purpleheart patio table and chairs. The only thing I did was add the workshop and renovate the kitchen and bathrooms."

She pulled the water bottle to her and twisted it open. "Thanks. Didn't realize I was thirsty until I saw this."

He nodded as she took a sip, then grudgingly said, "If you're hungry, there's some venison stew in the refrigerator, plenty enough to share. I've got fresh fruit, things for salad, too, if you want."

She set the bottle down and crossed her arms on the tabletop. "It's crystal clear that you don't want me here, and yet you offer me food and drinks and welcome me into your cozy, warm cabin. Which man is the real Aidan O'Brien? The one who can't help but act the host even when he doesn't want any visitors, and offers safety tips, or the one who committed murder and went to prison for ten years?"

He winced and set his beer down. "No beating around the bush with you. You go right for the jugular."

"I don't know any easy way to ease into asking you about your wife's death."

He briefly closed his eyes, then sat back in his chair and crossed his arms. "You obviously read my record. Everything is in my files. Why do you want me to talk about it?"

"Because I want your perspective, your side of it, not what police officers and lawyers summarized in their reports. You've lived most of your life in Nashville, right? That's where you met Elly?"

He sighed deeply, then cleared his throat. "Her name was Elly Larsen back then." He cleared his throat again. "My parents came here from Dublin when I was a teenager. That's the Irish brogue you mentioned. They moved several times until they settled in Nashville, bought a house two doors down from the Larsens. Our parents became best friends. Elly and I naturally became friends, too. That lasted through high school, then college where we began dating. A few years after graduation, once I had my furniture-making venture up and running, we got married."

"Furniture-making. You started your own business right out of college?"

"Pretty much. My grandparents on both sides were woodworkers all their lives. Although my father wasn't into that, I was fascinated by the stories my grandparents told and loved the carpentry and carving projects they involved me in whenever they visited. The only reason I went to college was to learn about running a business so I could start mine as soon as possible."

"Judging by this cabin, the sixty-plus acres that you bought with it, your business must have done really well."

"It's eighty-plus now that I bought out the only other neighbor on top of this mountain. You really did read up on me."

"That's part of my job."

He shrugged and took another sip of beer.

"How long was it before you and Elly had your son, Niall?"

He stared at her a long moment before answering. "He was born seven months after we got married. Elly lied during the entire pregnancy to her parents, telling them she wasn't as far along as she was. When he was born she swore to them that he was a preemie. She didn't want them to know we'd slept together before marriage. Considering that Niall was eight pounds at birth, and her parents weren't stupid, they obviously only pretended to believe her to help her save face."

"They sound like loving parents, not wanting their daughter to be embarrassed that she didn't follow tradition, or perhaps her religious beliefs."

"Both, and yes, they were loving, good people. Still are."

"Where's your son now?"

He glanced sharply at her. "With Elly's parents, my former in-laws."

"Did your parents try for custody?"

His throat tightened. "No. They had me late in life and weren't in the best of health when…all of this began. They didn't want to start over with a young child. They left the raising of Niall to the Larsens and moved back to Ireland when I went to prison."

Her eyes widened. "I'm so sorry. For your son, and for you."

"Don't be. My parents are…different. I know they care… about both of us. It's been difficult on them and they needed help I was no longer around to provide. They're with extended family and do what they can to keep in touch long-distance."

"So then Niall is with the Larsens full-time."

"Yes. The court terminated my parental rights and Elly's parents adopted him. My lawyer sends my child support payments to their lawyer and provides basic updates on Niall's health. But that's it."

"Child support. He's not an adult yet?"

"Almost. He turned seventeen back in the spring."

"So when your wife died, he was—"

"Five years old. I doubt he even remembers me. I hope to hell his grandparents are keeping his mother's memory alive for him. She deserves that." He took another swig of his beer and eyed the whiskey on the bar in the great room, longing for something stronger.

"Elly's parents didn't bring your son to visit you while you were incarcerated?"

"Why would they after what…what I did? I wouldn't

have wanted them to even if they'd offered. Prison is no place for a child."

"So you've never seen him, not even after you got out a year ago?"

"Twelve months and ten days ago. Aside from an annual picture the Larsens' lawyer sends my lawyer, I haven't seen Niall since the day the Larsens took him away. My lawyer has made an open invitation that if Niall ever wants to meet me, the lawyer will arrange a supervised visit on neutral grounds. But I doubt his grandparents have ever even passed the invitation along. I can't blame them. He's better off without me in his life. Dredging up old memories, a painful past, wouldn't do him any good." He crossed his arms again.

"I'm sorry. About your son."

"It is what it is. But…thanks."

She leaned forward, her gaze searching his. "I know this is difficult, but could you tell me about the night of the fire?"

He winced and shoved back from the table. "Give me a minute." He strode into the main part of the great room and stood in front of the large picture window that framed the incredible beauty of the Smoky Mountains in the distance.

When Malone joined him, quietly standing beside him as he looked out the window, he couldn't help putting off the discussion about the fire just a little longer. Instead, he told her, "Elly loved the mountains. She wanted to spend our honeymoon in a cabin in Gatlinburg. I wanted to take a cruise, soak up the sun on a beach. We went to Gatlinburg. How could I not? It made her happy. And she was pregnant with our first…" He swallowed. "With our only child. It's the least I could do. She was already experiencing morning sickness. It was easier on her to be pampered on the back deck of a mountain cabin than to sit out in the hot sun by the ocean."

He could feel her staring at him and he shifted uncomfortably.

"Your voice changes when you talk about her," she said. "You loved her, didn't you?"

He frowned. "Of course I did. That's why I…why I let her go."

"Because of the fire."

He nodded.

"Tell me what happened. Please."

He drew a shaky breath, then motioned toward one of the couches. "I need to sit down for this."

Once they were seated, to his surprise, she helped him ease into the conversation about that awful night by talking about more mundane things that really didn't matter. She asked about his business, things he and Elly did, the first few years of life as young parents with a rambunctious son running them ragged.

"Earlier you mentioned your parents try to keep in touch, even from Ireland. What about your grandparents? Or are they all gone now?"

"If by gone you mean have they passed away, no. They're all remarkably healthy for their ages, doing really well. But after I…confessed…they cut me out of their lives. I'm an only child, no siblings. The only family who speaks to me these days is my parents, and then, only rarely. As I said, they aren't in the best of health."

"I'm sorry."

He glanced at her, surprised to hear the empathy in her voice, see the sorrow in her eyes. He gave her a curt nod of thanks and looked away again, staring toward the mountains, which were beginning to mist over, giving them the smoky look for which they'd been named.

"We'd only been in the house for a few weeks," he finally began. "The business had taken off. I was making millions, investing the profits and making millions on top of that. I never expected the high-end custom furniture market to be that lucrative and successful. But it was. I took it international and it really exploded. I had over a hundred people working for me at the time, far more now in several locations around the world. In spite of that, all Elly wanted was a slightly bigger house than our starter home so we'd have room for more children. But I wanted a statement home, something grand that reinforced the image of success."

He shook his head in disgust. "My ego and pride had me overrule her desires that one time and insist on getting a mansion in the foothills outside of Nashville in one of the upper-crust neighborhoods. It was huge, beautiful, but old. The inspection pointed out dozens of things that needed to be upgraded. One of those was the electrical system. It was original to the house and the inspector warned it wasn't capable of handling all the modern smart appliances and technological toys that people have these days. We could have waited, had the electrical completely redone before we moved in. But I didn't take the inspector's warnings seriously enough. I thought we had time, that we could do the renovations after we were settled."

He shook his head in self-disgust. "Obviously, I was wrong. I was working late one night at my company, meeting with my more senior craftsmen about new equipment and tools they felt we needed. Once all of that was wrapped up, it was past the dinner hour and dark outside. I could see the flames lighting up the night sky before I even turned down our street. Firefighters and police officers were everywhere, lights flashing, hoses pouring water onto the second story of our home. I jumped out of my car and tried to run inside, but they held me back. I screamed at them that my wife and son were in there. One of the policemen told me they'd been rescued, that my son was fine and with a neighbor, but that my wife was at the hospital."

He squeezed his hands into fists. "*Rescued.* That word scared the hell out of me. What did it mean? I was afraid to ask. I checked on Niall, then sped to the hospital. Once there I…" He closed his eyes, reliving the nightmare yet again as the horrible images bombarded his mind.

"Elly," he whispered, his eyes still closed. "My God. Elly."

She was in the burn unit, soot and burns over large swaths of her body. But it was her silence that was more terrifying than screams of pain would have been.

"Aidan?"

He opened his eyes, glad that the agent had brought him back from the darkness. Not that he'd thank her for it. "I told you to call me Mr. O'Brien."

"And I told you to call me Grace."

He couldn't help but smile at that. Then he blew out a shaky breath and gave her a sanitized version of what Elly had suffered.

"The fire started upstairs. An electrical short. Elly was downstairs and heard Niall screaming. She ran and didn't realize there was a fire until she reached the landing. Flames were between her and our son's room. She ran right through them to get him. She…she grabbed the comforter off his bed and soaked it in the shower, then covered both of them as she ran through the flames again to the stairs. They'd just reached the bottom when a beam fell on her. Niall was able to scramble out from under her and run outside. The firefighters had to pull the beam off her and take her out."

Malone gave him another one of those empathetic smiles he didn't begin to deserve. "She was paralyzed, correct?"

"From the chest down. She had to be on a ventilator to breathe. After months of treatment in the burn center, she was well enough to go home. But the vent was permanent. She'd die without it. She had partial use of her right arm, and she could turn her head, blink her eyes. Little else. In some ways the paralysis was a blessing because she didn't suffer as much as she would have during burn treatments. But she'd have traded the pain to be able to walk again, to breathe on her own, to hold her son."

"How do you know that?"

"She told me."

"I thought she had a ventilator. Doesn't that prevent you from speaking?"

"Her ventilator was connected to her trachea. Her mouth wasn't covered. And it had this…valve, a…Passy Muir Valve. That's what it was called. It helped her speak. She could write a little, too, with her right hand. But it was really difficult. She preferred the valve."

"I didn't read about that in the reports in your file."

He shrugged. "I don't know that it matters either way. Why do you keep asking these—"

"Let's skip to the last day of her life, seven months after the accident."

"Surely those details are in the police reports."

"Not as much as I'd expect. The investigative file is surprisingly sparse. Even though it was several months after her death before you were brought to court, there doesn't seem to have been much of an investigation."

"Why would there be? I told the police what happened. When the day nurse who watched over Elly whenever I was at work left, I unplugged my wife's ventilator. I let her go." He swallowed, his throat tight as he struggled to keep his composure.

Rather than accept his confession, Malone frowned as if she was weighing it for the truth. "From what I've read, there are alarms on the machine that was keeping your wife alive. If you unplugged it, the backup battery—as long as it was charged and working correctly—would have kicked in to keep the machine going until it was plugged in again or the battery died. The particular model your wife used has ten minutes of battery life. Alarms would have been going off that whole time."

He hesitated. "Right. They were. I knew all about the alarms. I was trained to use her equipment, to suction, clean, keep it going if any alarms went off during the night while there weren't any nurses there watching over her. Again, why do you feel you need to—"

"Aidan. You ran into the woods this morning with no way to defend yourself against a man with a lethal weapon. You risked your life because you didn't want him to shoot an arrow near strangers, people who weren't your loved ones. Do you honestly expect me to believe that you unplugged your wife's machine, your son's mother, and sat there for the ten minutes for the battery to run down with all those alarms going off, then several more minutes watching her struggle until she died, before finally calling 911?"

His face flushed with heat. His pulse raced and he could feel a bead of sweat running down his back.

"Aidan?"

"I don't expect you to believe anything. And I don't care whether you do or not. I confessed to my crime, went to prison. Why does it even matter at this point?"

"Your son was in the house at the time?"

Good grief, she was tenacious. And getting far too close to the truth. He needed her to stop digging. That was the only reason he hung on, continued answering her questions as he desperately tried to assuage her curiosity and convince her, somehow, to let it go. To move on to something else, to someone else, in her investigation.

"Yes," he finally said. "He was in his room, playing."

"Did he come into his mother's room when he heard the alarms?"

Another bead of sweat raced down his back. "He… No, he stayed in his room." At her look of disbelief, he quickly added, "He'd gone on a field trip that day with his kindergarten class, to the zoo. He was worn-out, fell asleep as soon as I got him home. His door was shut, and…Elly's door was shut."

"I see. How far away was your son's room from Elly's?"

His throat ached with the urge to shout at her. *Stop. Please. Just, stop.*

"Far enough that he didn't hear anything. And I… Right, I silenced the machine. I forgot about that. I turned off the alarms."

"You just said the alarms were going off. Now you're saying you turned them off."

He stood. "I've answered your questions, far more than I should have to, given that none of this even remotely touches on your investigation into the serial killer you're looking for. It's time for you to go."

She stood and looked up at him. "I know this has been difficult. But I appreciate your cooperation. There is one more thing, though. It's not about your wife. Earlier today, you told me that you use a bow and arrows to hunt. Can you show them to me?"

He swore beneath his breath. "I always keep a bow and quiver of arrows in my truck. You can look at those on your way out. It's parked beside the cabin. My other equipment is in here." He headed to the first bedroom under the stairs. He flung open the door and headed into the closet to grab his bow and one of the quivers of arrows to give her. But when he turned around, she was standing in the closet doorway.

"I need to verify for myself," she said unapologetically.

He tossed the bow and arrows down and left the room.

A few minutes later, she joined him by the front door. "I don't see anything remotely resembling a crossbow anywhere. And as you said earlier, your arrows are longer, without any white feathers for fletching. Oh, wait, that was another question I had, about the fletching."

He opened the door and leaned against the frame. "Make it quick. My patience is at an end."

"It's what you were saying at the station during our earlier interview, before Dawson cut it short. I was talking about the arrows from the incident at this morning's festival. I said the fletching was both plastic and feathers. You corrected me, said that the arrows you saw… What? What were you going to add to that?"

He frowned, trying to remember, then nodded. "Right. I think I was making the point that the plastic on the arrows was the fletching, for the aerodynamics. That's a crucial part of the arrow to make it fly straight and true. The feather isn't fletching, not the one dangling from the arrow. That wouldn't help stabilize the shot. It would wreak havoc on the aerodynamics. Anyone shooting a bow and arrow using a large feather off the end like that isn't concerned with accuracy."

Her eyes widened. "Meaning whoever he shoots just happens to be in the way of the arrow. He's not really aiming."

"Exactly."

She swore. "We've been focusing too much on victimology, trying to dig into the backgrounds of our victims and figure out what links them together. The answer to that is—"

"Nothing," he said. "Wrong time. Wrong place. The victims are random. Unless he attaches the feathers after he shoots someone. I suppose that's possible, too. Then you're back to looking at victimology."

Some of her excitement drained out of her. "True. Well, it's another angle to look into, regardless. Thank you, Aidan. You've been extremely helpful." She held out her hand.

He sighed heavily. Her use of his first name was a technique to build a connection with him so he'd answer questions. He knew it. But dang if it wasn't working to some extent. Feeling spiteful at this point if he again refused to shake her hand, he shook it. And immediately felt his anger draining away. Her soft, warm touch was like a soothing balm over the wounds in his soul that had been reopened during the interrogation. That simple human contact that he normally avoided sparked a stirring in his heart that he'd thought had died years ago. He quickly broke the contact out of desperation and self-preservation. He didn't want the man he used to be to wake up, to feel everything so deeply and painfully again. He needed to lock away that part of himself just to survive.

She gave him a sad smile as if she understood what he was thinking. And that scared the hell out of him.

"Aidan, I know there's more to what happened the night your wife died than you've ever admitted. Whatever it is that you're holding back, remember that the law can't punish you a second time for the same crime. You've served your time. Have you considered that telling the truth will unburden your conscience, lift a terrible weight off your shoulders and allow you to finally begin the healing process?"

He motioned toward the open door. "Goodbye, Special Agent Malone."

She sighed and headed outside.

The sound of another car engine and wheels crunching on gravel had him stepping onto the porch to see what was going on. As Malone was walking toward her car, one of the police station's Jeeps was heading toward her.

"How did I get so lucky today?" Aidan muttered.

The unmistakable sound of an arrow whistling through the air had him shouting a warning.

"Hit the deck!"

Malone dived to the ground a split second *after* the arrow embedded itself in the back of her SUV, with a large white feather dangling from the end. If the arrow had been a little to the left, it would have driven deep into her back.

Aidan whirled around just in time to see someone disappearing into the woods on the far side of the cabin. He immediately took off after them.

"Freeze, or I'll shoot!" Dawson's voice rang out.

Aidan slid to a halt and slowly raised his hands.

Chapter Seven

"I'm fine, I'm fine," Grace yelled as Dawson stopped to check on her. "Go! Get him!"

Dawson ran past her, past the front of the cabin and into the woods. Grace climbed painfully to her feet, flicking off the worst of the gravel that had dug into her legs through the tears they'd made in her pants. But she didn't have time to feel sorry for herself. Ignoring the stinging in her skinned knees, she yanked her pistol out of her holster and jogged up the porch steps to check on Aidan.

"Are you okay? No arrows hit you, did they?" she asked.

He slowly turned and lowered his hands, a look of confusion on his face. "You're not arresting me?"

She frowned. "Arrest you? Why would I do that?"

"I figured you both thought I was the…" He shook his head, seemingly stunned. "You saw the shooter?"

"Dawson did. He's on his trail right now. And I need to back him up. Lock yourself in your cabin and—"

"Hell, no. I'm not hiding while some fool runs around on my property playing cowboys and Indians, not caring whether he hurts someone, or worse." He took off across the porch.

"Wait. That's an order!"

"I'm not one of your agents to boss around." He took the stairs two at a time, then sprinted toward the woods where Dawson had gone.

Grace said a few unsavory words and took off after both of them. As she ran, she called the station and updated Fletcher about what was happening. Fletcher promised she'd rally the troops. Grace ended the call and slowed, realizing she'd already lost the trail. She searched the ground, trying her best to track where the suspect, Dawson, and Aidan had gone.

She loved mountain views and outdoors as much as most living in the beautiful state of Tennessee. But that didn't mean she was Danielle Boone. She'd never gone hunting or camping, and her version of roughing it was a three-star motel. Trying to figure out which way someone had gone, by looking for shoe prints or bent grass or whatever, was proving to be beyond her skills.

She finally gave up and tried calling Dawson, but he didn't answer his phone. Another call to Officer Fletcher got Aidan's cell phone number from his police folder. Grace punched it in, but like the police chief, he didn't pick up.

Worried they might be in trouble, she kept going, desperately hoping she was headed the right way. A few minutes later, the sound of male voices had her stopping again. There, up ahead through a break in the trees, she saw Dawson and Aidan. Side by side, shoulder to shoulder, they were jogging in her direction. They weren't smiling or laughing. But they weren't arguing or exchanging blows either. They almost seemed…friendly. She was so surprised that she forgot for a second why the three of them had gone into the woods to begin with.

She never saw the second arrow coming.

"I'M FINE. Stop fussing over me," Grace assured Aidan and the chief for the dozenth time as she sat beside them on one of Aidan's couches. Kneeling in front of her was Officer Collier. Apparently, he served as one of the town's part-time EMTs in addition to his police duties. "The arrow barely touched me, just a scratch. Doesn't even need stitches."

Collier shook his head. "Actually, I'm having trouble getting the bleeding to stop. I may have to stitch it closed."

Her face flushed. "Seriously? Isn't there a doctor around here who can do it?"

"Nope. But if you're squeamish, I can put a pressure bandage on it for now and take you to the hospital."

"The hospital? Where is that?"

"The other side of Chattanooga. About an hour and a half away."

"Good grief. What do you people do around here for something really serious?"

"Helicopter," Dawson told her. "The town purchased a used medevac chopper last year after a little girl nearly died because it took so long to get her to the hospital. An anonymous donation put us over the top on our fundraiser and we had enough money left over to stock it with medical supplies and train several key people in town as EMTs, including Collier."

Remembering how worried Aidan had been this morning about children being in harm's way, and knowing he had money to spare, she glanced at him beside her, wondering if he could be that anonymous donor. But he didn't react, gave no indication either way.

Dawson leaned around Aidan to get a better look at Grace's injured arm.

Aidan shoved him back. "Give your guy room to work. He needs to get that bleeding under control."

Dawson narrowed his eyes, but didn't retaliate over the shove. That was amazing since if Aidan had shoved him this morning he'd have likely been thrown in jail. They must have come to some kind of agreement in the woods earlier to set aside their mutual differences and suspicions. Maybe it was because they'd agreed to work together toward the common goal of finding whoever was terrorizing this town.

"Chief Dawson," Grace asked, "in all the chaos that's happened, I never got a chance to ask why you came up here in the first place."

"Yet another anonymous tip. A man called to say that a woman was here visiting O'Brien and that she might be in trouble. And before you say it, yes, I know how thin that is. Considering that's the first anonymous tip I've ever gotten—"

"Mine, too," Grace said. "Although the tip was to the FBI, not me specifically. I listened to the recording, of course."

"Was the FBI tipster male?"

"He was," she said. "But his voice was tinny, like he was using a device to alter the sound of his real voice. We put a trace on the call, but it led to a burner phone, a throwaway. We've still got people on it, but so far no luck in identifying who made the call."

"I'll see what kind of trace we can do, too, after we're done here."

Aidan glanced back and forth between them. "Hold it. You're saying an anonymous caller sent the FBI here looking for this Crossbow Killer, and another caller sent the police here to my place. Then, both times someone shot an arrow from over my shoulder, making it appear that I was the one who'd shot it. Does that smell like a setup to you?"

"Yes," they both said.

"And it was a good one," the chief added. "Because if one of the townspeople hadn't taken a picture of their family at the festival and it captured you in the background, with that arrow zinging past you, I'd likely still have you locked up. Likewise, when I drove up here, if I hadn't seen a shadow behind you shooting that first arrow at Malone, I'd have locked you up then, too. The game this guy's playing isn't turning out the way he hoped. Instead of convincing us of your guilt, he's done the opposite. You're the real victim here." He glanced at Grace. "One of them, anyway."

"It's just a scratch," she repeated.

He rolled his eyes again.

"O'Brien," Grace said, purposely using his last name in front of the others. "Do you have any idea who would hate you enough to try to frame you as a serial killer?"

His jaw tightened. "I would think my in-laws despise me. How could they not? We never got a chance to speak after I was arrested. They were grieving, too upset and shocked to seek me out. I sent an apology, again, through my lawyer. But how do you apologize for something like that? Regardless, I can't see them coming after me, or even having someone else do it on their behalf. They're truly good, decent people. They just… No, it's not them."

"There has to be someone else, then. Help us make a list." This time it was Chief Dawson who spoke. "If not your former in-laws, then who? Who else could it be?"

Aidan thought for a moment, then shook his head. "No one. I mean, there are plenty of people who'd love to see me dead based on the hate mail I received in prison. But they were strangers, people who get fired up over news reports. I can't imagine any of them actually coming after me all these years later."

"Do you still have those letters?" Grace asked.

He hesitated, his gaze capturing hers. He was silent for several moments.

"Do you?"

He looked away. "I threw them out. They certainly weren't comforting or sentimental, something to take with me to reread after I was released. No. I don't have the letters."

Grace didn't believe him. That hesitation told her he was holding something back. Was there someone who'd written him that he'd just realized might be the one trying to frame him? If so, why not tell them?

Dawson leaned forward to get Aidan's attention. "What about people here in Mystic Lake? Other than the obvious—people being wary of you because of your past—has anyone gone out of their way to antagonize you? Have you made any enemies?"

This time, he didn't hesitate. "No. I can count on one hand the friends I've made here, with a couple of fingers left over. But I keep to myself for the most part and haven't made any enemies. I'm sure that, like other strangers who heard about my case, many of the townspeople wish I'd go live somewhere else. They likely have strong feelings against me. But again, to go this far, to frame me and risk the lives of innocent people over what they think I…" He cleared his throat. "For what I did, I can't think of anyone who would do that."

Grace stared at him, the words he'd stumbled over running through her mind. *For what they think I… For what I did.* Was he going to say for what they thought he did? Had he slipped up and almost admitted that he *didn't* kill his wife? She noted that Dawson and Collier were both studying Aidan, too, as if weighing the words he'd just said and realizing there might be more to his past, a truth no one else knew. Except Aidan.

Aidan cleared his throat and stood. "Anyone need a drink?" He headed into the kitchen side of the large, open room.

Hoping to break the tension that had fallen over everyone, Grace called out, "Yes, please. The coldest beer you have. None of that light stuff, either."

"No way," Collier said. "We're all on duty, including you. And you're my patient. I won't be able to give you any pain medicine if you drink."

"Meanie."

He laughed.

Still debating whether or not to allow a part-time, relatively new EMT to stick a needle in her arm to stitch her up, she asked Collier, "Who flies the helicopter?"

He pressed some fresh gauze against her arm, mumbling an apology when she winced. "Bobby Thompson. He's—"

"The owner of the marina. I remember you told me earlier."

"He's also retired military, flew a chopper for most of his career. He oversees the maintenance and flies when needed. Stella Holman, from the bed-and-breakfast, was a career nurse before vacationing here, then meeting Frank, getting married and staying for good. She's the one who rides with Bobby to take care of the patients until they reach the hospital."

A loud knock on the open door of the cabin had all of

them looking over to see Officer Fletcher standing there. "Justin's arrived with his scent dog."

"About time," Dawson said. He stood and Aidan met him at the door.

Dawson arched a brow. "Don't even think about it. You might not be a suspect anymore, but you're still a civilian."

"Who saved you from tumbling over a cliff's edge earlier. Remember that?"

Dawson's face reddened. Now Grace understood why the chief was treating Aidan more like a friend than a foe. She could well imagine how much he loathed owing his life to an ex-con. Judging by the hard set of his jaw, he didn't like it one bit.

Aidan continued. "It's my land. I know the best ways to get through the brush, where the slopes have loose rocks and dangerous footing, where the cliffs—"

"Okay, okay. You made your point," Dawson grumbled. "You can go, but only as a guide. If we find this guy, don't make any attempts to intervene or take him down. That's for the police to do. Understood?"

Aidan crossed his arms.

Dawson swore but didn't waste more time arguing. "Let's go, while we still have daylight left." He strode onto the front porch where Fletcher, Ortiz, and the man with the scent dog were waiting.

Aidan grabbed the door to pull it closed behind him, then hesitated. "Collier, don't let Special Agent Malone out of your sight. I expect she'll want to head after us again after you patch her up. But if the shooter is still in the area, he might try to finish what he started. Under no circumstances allow her through this door."

"Yes, sir," Collier called out.

Aidan pulled the door shut.

Grace blinked in shock. "Did you just take orders from an ex-con?"

Collier snorted. "Emphasis on ex. He served his time. And I'm not convinced he was ever guilty to begin with."

"He confessed."

"With all due respect, Malone, I'm not one of those officers who thinks everyone in prison is guilty. Innocent people do get convicted sometimes, probably more than most people realize. They make false confessions. It's a proven fact. New evidence, like DNA, has exonerated plenty of them."

"You think his confession was false?"

"Let me put it this way. The chief has accused him of just about every petty crime that happens around here since the day O'Brien came to Mystic Lake. He hasn't exactly made it easy on the guy. Then we get proof he's being framed. And even though O'Brien has every reason to want payback against Dawson, when the chief's foot slips and he could have fallen to his death, O'Brien risked his own life to grab him and haul him back to safety."

"Dawson told you that? I mean, I heard Aidan say something about it but I didn't know any details."

"When I got here, he told me what happened, yeah."

"I get what you're saying," she said. "But what makes you so certain he wasn't a different person years ago, that he didn't kill his wife? Did he tell you he didn't?"

"Ever heard of a Freudian slip? That's what he did earlier, if you ask me. He basically admitted he didn't kill his wife. You heard that too, right?"

"Yes. I did."

"So did Dawson. We've all wondered about O'Brien,

played devil's advocate about how he could kill his wife. If you read his case file you'll see interviews the prosecutor did with people who knew him. And pretty much every one of them said he and his wife were wild about each other and that if he did take her life it was out of mercy. You know about the fire, right? That she was paralyzed and in terrible pain."

"Yes, but that doesn't excuse killing her. That's not how our society and our laws work."

He gave her a hard look, then shrugged. "Whatever happened, he's not the bad guy people think he is. Not even close. He may be gruff, rude sometimes. Okay, rude a lot of times. But that's how he protects himself. If you don't let people in, they can't hurt you, you know? Anyway, my point is that he's never, not once, done anything to hurt anyone around here. Just the opposite. He doesn't advertise it or try to take credit, but he helps people all the time."

She was stunned to hear a police officer speaking about Aidan this way, particularly an officer who'd helped another lock him to a conference room table this morning. "How does he help people?"

He swore when he pulled the latest gauze off her arm and it came away bloody. He grabbed a fresh one and pressed hard.

She forced herself to hold still and not give any indication about how much he was hurting her. He was a gold mine of information and she didn't want him to stop talking.

"Collier, how does Aidan help people?"

"Oh, you know. Lots of ways. You've heard about the town's, the lake's, reputation, right? Unexplained things happen around here. Mysterious deaths, disappearances, strange accidents. I mean, we really do have a lot of wacky stuff that goes on. Did you know Mystic Lake has more drownings per year than any other lake in the country?"

"You're kidding. Why? What makes it so dangerous?"

"If you ask the townsfolk, most will tell you it's the spirits of the people who drowned in the lake when the superstorm came through decades ago and flooded this place."

"For real, Collier. What makes the lake so dangerous?"

"Because of the flood."

"Collier—"

"No, no, I'm not talking about ghosts. I'm serious. I'm talking about what's underneath the water. An entire town is at the bottom of the lake. Houses, cars, church spires, trees, lots and lots of dead trees. We do cleanups every year. Hundreds of volunteers pull out debris so boats and swimmers won't get hung up in all that stuff on the bottom. But some of it is too deep to reach. And the lake is huge. Not the part downtown, but the part outside of town by the marina. It's impossible to clean it all. We post warning signs in areas where drownings or boating accidents have occurred, and focus on those areas during our cleanups. Tourists are warned. Locals are reminded all the time about the dangers. But the lake is beautiful, and relatively safe if you stay within the markers. So people come here in droves in the summer to enjoy it. But things still happen."

"Okay. But what does any of this have to do with Aidan?"

"Since when did you start referring to him by his first name?"

Her stomach tightened as she rushed to cover her mistake. "Since I started trying to build rapport in search of the truth. You were saying?"

He gave her a suspicious look, as if he didn't believe

her. But he continued. "He's one of the main sponsors on cleanup days, pays to have salvage boats come in and take out debris in the more dangerous areas. And, last summer, on one of those rare days when he showed up around the crowds, he ended up saving some swimmers. They got hung up in some sunken tree branches. He dived in before anyone even realized the swimmers were in trouble, got them free. One of them wasn't breathing when O'Brien pulled her out. He performed CPR until she was breathing again. But it was touch and go for quite a while."

"The little girl who almost died, before the chopper was here?"

He nodded. "And that's not all. There are other things. Like, if someone can't pay their rent, suddenly an envelope of money appears in their mailbox. And the anonymous donor of the chopper money like you said. Nothing like that ever happened around here until he showed up. I can't be sure what exactly occurred in his past with his wife. But I am sure of one thing. The man he is today is a good man. And I trust him more than I'd trust half the people here in town who makc themselves out to be way better than they actually are."

The silence stretched out between them.

His face reddened as if everything he'd said was already coming back to haunt him. "It must be because you're an FBI agent that my mouth got the better of me. You tell the chief I said any of that and I'll deny it. He wouldn't take kindly to one of his officers, as you said earlier, talking that way about an ex-con."

She shifted slightly forward on the couch. "I won't tell if you don't tell him about me."

He frowned. "What do you mean?"

"I have the same doubts about Aidan as you." She winced and motioned toward his hand on her arm. "Unless you're trying to completely cut off all circulation, you think you could ease up there?"

"What? Oh, sorry." His face reddened again as he reduced the pressure. "That bleeding isn't going to stop on its own."

"Stitches?"

"Stitches. I'll get that pressure bandage in place and drive you to the hospital."

"Heck, no. I'm not riding in a car for over an hour for two stitches."

"More like three. Maybe even four."

She blinked. "Four?" She craned her neck to try to see the underside of her arm.

He pushed her back against the couch. "Stop worrying. I'll give you a shot of painkiller first. You won't feel a thing."

"Except the shot," she grumbled.

He laughed and, a little too eagerly for her peace of mind, reached for a hypodermic needle in his medical bag.

Chapter Eight

Grace stood at the largest picture window in Aidan's cabin, staring out at the rapidly darkening sky. "They've been gone too long. And once again no one's answering their cell phones."

"Standard operating procedure," Collier called out from the kitchen. "Radio silence while hunting a suspect. Or, in this case, phone silence. Hey, looks like some venison stew's in here. You think O'Brien would mind if we had some? I'm starving."

"Accepting drinks from a civilian is one thing. Eating up their food is another."

"I skipped dinner."

"So did I." She headed for the door. "I'm going to check on them and see if they—"

He was suddenly in front of her, his back to the door. "If you want to find out whether I'm more afraid of you or my boss, trust me. Dawson trumps you any time."

She flipped her jacket back, revealing her holster. "I have a gun."

He snorted. "Mine's bigger."

"Oh, good grief. I know karate, Collier. Don't make me hurt you."

"You've got four stitches in your arm and it has to be sore. Besides, your black belt doesn't scare me. I weigh twice what you do, at least. All I have to do is sit on you and—oof!"

Grace stood over him where she'd flipped him onto his back. "Can't say I didn't warn you."

"Nope," he groaned. "Can't say you didn't. If you ripped your stitches out don't ask me to patch you up again. You hurt my feelings." He grimaced. "And my back."

"I'll buy you a day at the spa." She headed to the door again and threw it open.

Aidan stood in the opening, arching a brow. "Going somewhere?"

She groaned. "Great timing."

He looked past her. "Seriously, Collier? You're twice her size. And she's injured. Did she put you on the floor?"

"Afraid so." He groaned again. "I might need help getting up."

Aidan stepped inside, forcing Grace to back up. He stopped beside Collier, shaking his head. "Pathetic." He grabbed Collier's hand and hauled him upright.

"Ouch, sheesh. Some warning would have been nice, man."

"Twice her size, Collier," Aidan reminded him. "Unbelievable." He headed into the kitchen and opened the door to what must have been his pantry.

"Trust me," Collier said. "I won't underestimate her again." He gave Grace a hurt look and limped to the couch. "Not that I should be nice to you after that, but I meant to tell you earlier to keep your bandage dry when you shower. I'll need to change it tomorrow and make sure an infection isn't setting in. Just promise you won't flip me over your shoulder again."

"That depends on whether you deserve it or not," she teased.

He rolled his eyes. "Oh, hey, O'Brien. I saw some venison stew in your refrigerator earlier—"

"Collier," Grace warned.

He gave her a sullen look and settled deeper against the cushions.

"Where's everyone else, Aidan?" She moved toward the door again as he spread a checkered tablecloth over the table.

"Right here," a voice said.

She had to step back for Dawson and Fletcher to come inside. Dawson was carrying a quiver of arrows. Fletcher followed, wearing latex gloves and holding a quart-sized can and a brush with dried red paint on it. She set her bounty on the tabletop and gave Aidan an odd look when he sat at the table.

"Should you be here with the evidence?" she asked.

"Officer Fletcher," Dawson said. "Is there a reason the owner of this property, the victim in an attempted framing scheme who helped us find this evidence and is allowing us to temporarily use his home, shouldn't sit with us and discuss what we've found?"

Her face reddened. "No, sir."

"I didn't think so."

Aidan gave him a subtle nod of thanks.

Fletcher's face turned even redder. Obviously, she wasn't in the same camp as Collier, or even Dawson now, about Aidan's character.

Dawson set the quiver on the table and then made a

detour to the couch, looking down at Collier. "Do I even want to know?"

Collier grimaced. "No, sir."

Dawson shook his head and returned to the table, sitting beside Fletcher. Grace sat to Aidan's left. Collier made an amazing recovery and jogged over to take the chair between Aidan and Fletcher.

"What happened?" Grace asked. "Is Ortiz taking the suspect to jail?"

"No," Dawson said. "Ortiz is at the station. A 911 call came in while we were out so he had to rush back and take care of it. False alarm. Everyone's fine. But he'll hang there for now."

"So you didn't find the suspect, but you found his things in the woods?"

Aidan motioned toward the pile in the middle of the table. "The dog led us to a creek at the outer edge of my property. He lost the trail after that, likely because the suspect crossed the creek or maybe walked in it to help dilute his scent. We'd have split up and kept going, figuring we could catch up to him even without the dog's help. But it was getting dark, too dangerous. Most of my land has been left in its natural state."

"Meaning," Dawson added, "it's full of thick brush, downed trees and steep drop-offs. Far too dangerous in bad lighting. We'll search again tomorrow in case he comes back, or has hunkered down somewhere and never left. Speaking of which, O'Brien, you might want to stay at the B and B for a few days, at least until we catch this fool. Him shooting Malone when you were with me means he knows the game is up, that trying to frame you any longer isn't going to work. I think he took that first shot by the SUV to get us into the woods and give him time to get away. I'd rather you not be here alone without a gun to defend yourself if he comes back tonight."

"I can stay and guard him," Grace offered.

Aidan's jaw tightened. "I'm not going to cower behind—"

"A woman?" Grace snapped. "I'm perfectly capable of defending you, myself or anyone else."

Collier raised his hand. "I can attest to that."

"I was going to say that I'm not going to cower behind anyone else putting their lives on the line for me. I'll call Stella, see if there's a room available. If there is, I'll stay downtown for a few days. That should free up my cabin as a base of operations for the search tomorrow. I can give you a key, Dawson."

"I appreciate that. I'd also appreciate it if you help with the search. But only if we can keep you safe in the process. We'll discuss it in the morning."

"I'd definitely like to help," Aidan said.

"You don't have to call the B and B," Grace told him. "I reserved three rooms for the next three days. One is for me and the others are for more agents if I prove the real Crossbow Killer is operating here. We won't likely have that answer until the lab comparisons between the original arrows and the ones you found today come back. They're also running prints and DNA. I'll go online tomorrow and see if any results are ready. But I doubt it."

He nodded his thanks. "I'll pack a bag." He pushed up from the table and headed up the stairs.

Dawson motioned toward the arrows and the paintbrush. "I'm no expert, but these look the same to me as the ones from earlier. What's your take on these, Malone?"

"I didn't bring any gloves. Does anyone have a…" She laughed as all three of them offered her some latex gloves. "You run a tight ship, Dawson. Always be prepared, right?"

"Always."

She took the pair that Fletcher offered, thanking her as she pulled them on. Careful not to touch anything more than she had to, she picked the items up in the least likely places where the suspect might have touched them so that she could try to avoid destroying any viable latent prints.

After a careful examination, she set the evidence down and took a picture of the paint can to send to the lab, as well as the arrows.

"I can have this all couriered to the FBI lab tomorrow morning if you're okay with that."

"I was hoping you'd offer," Dawson said. "But I'd like to dust one of these arrows for prints locally to see if we get anything and put it into IAFIS. We've collected several arrows, so destroying any DNA on just one of them should be an acceptable trade-off to try to get a leg up and speed this along."

"I agree," she said. "For now, since we can't prove or disprove that the suspect is or isn't the Crossbow Killer, we can work on this as a team if, again Chief, you're okay with that."

"Absolutely. We've already set our other investigations aside to focus on this. The more resources we have the more likely we'll be to wrap this up sooner rather than later." He checked the time on his phone. "Speaking of later, it's been a long day for all of us. I recommend we head down the mountain and get a good night's sleep. We'll meet up early to continue the investigation."

"What about the search?" she asked. "You can't run an

investigation and a full-blown search at the same time. You need more people."

"Which is why I told Ortiz to contact the sheriff's office to get some bodies up here. Ortiz will be the liaison for our department and manage the search along with whoever Sheriff Galloway puts in charge from his side. He'll also make some casts of the shoe prints we found tonight. Justin will be here with his scent dog again, too. He already agreed to that. We have search-and-rescue volunteers we can call in a pinch. But this guy is dangerous and I don't want civilians out here as more innocent targets for him."

"Sounds like a well-thought-out plan. With Ortiz up here tomorrow, that leaves a desk free at your station. Mind if I operate out of there? I've got my own laptop and can show you the results as soon as the lab uploads them to our portal."

"Of course. Use anything you need. If you want the conference room, consider it yours, as well."

Fletcher grinned. "You might prefer the conference room, honestly. Ortiz is a bit of a slob. You'd be wiping crumbs off your nice blouse and slacks."

Grace looked down, making a face at her clothes. "They used to be nice. That tumble on the gravel driveway earlier pretty much ruined them. But I brought several more changes of clothes with me."

Fletcher gave her a commiserating look and stood. "Since Ortiz was my ride up here, boss, I'm going to have to bum a ride back with you."

"What about me?" Collier asked. "I can give you a ride."

"I'll ride with the boss." Fletcher made a face at Collier as she gathered up the paint can and brush again.

He rolled his eyes.

Aidan jogged down the stairs and joined them, a black leather overnight bag slung over his shoulder. "Special Agent Malone, I'll follow you to the B and B if that's all right, so you can let Stella know I'm taking one of those rooms you reserved."

"Since we're going to the same place, why not leave your truck here and ride with me?" she asked.

He glanced at Dawson. "I think it would be better if I take my truck. I'll need it in the morning. But thanks."

Grace realized all three of the police officers were looking at her. Fletcher was obviously no fan of Aidan. Dawson was grudgingly coming around, but his expression clearly said he didn't think it was appropriate for her to ride with a felon convicted of murder. Even Collier seemed surprised that a federal agent, no doubt especially a woman in this situation, would be so lax.

"Right," she said, her face heating. "That makes more sense. I'll meet you at the front desk." She couldn't seem to get out of the cabin and to her car fast enough.

Good grief, what was she doing? It was one thing to believe that a man was innocent and feel comfortable around him. But she was an FBI agent. She knew better than to allow emotions to override good judgment. Something about Aidan called out to her on a primal level, and it wasn't just that he was, well, hot. Really hot. That shouldn't matter, not right now. What mattered was maintaining her professionalism and following her training. This was her first time out solo. She couldn't screw it up.

Chapter Nine

Grace stood at the front desk, watching Aidan enter the lobby of the B and B. She'd already notified the young man at the front desk that Aidan would be taking one of the rooms that she'd reserved. Aidan signed the register. Then she and Aidan headed upstairs.

At the top landing, she pointed to the room across the hall from hers. "That one's yours. But before you go inside, I'd like to ask you something."

His expression turned wary. "Go ahead."

"At your cabin, when I asked about the hate mail you received in prison and whether you kept it, you hesitated. Is that because you threw away most of it, but kept some? Are you protecting someone by not telling the whole truth?"

He leaned against the wall beside her door, his overnight bag still slung over his shoulder. "What are your plans in the morning?" he asked.

"You're changing the subject."

"Yes. I am. I already answered your question earlier. Now answer mine. What are your plans in the morning?"

"My plans. Are we talking…breakfast? Together?" Her stomach tightened with a mixture of pleasure and dread. Was he asking her out? If so, she'd have to put the kibosh on it. She'd already screwed up royally tonight in front of other law enforcement officers. She had to be careful or something would get back to her boss. He'd order her back to Knoxville and it would be months before she'd be allowed to fly solo again.

He smiled. "The restaurant downstairs is the main one for the town. It's a large open room with tables fairly close together to accommodate the crowds. I certainly wouldn't mind sitting with you, but given the circumstances, that's not a good idea."

"Aidan, I—"

"You need to start calling me O'Brien again. Even if you think you can trust me, most people, like Officer Fletcher, don't. It can't be good for your reputation to be seen on friendly terms with an ex-con."

"You're actually worried about my reputation? Just this morning I was trying to nail you as the Crossbow Killer."

"Which only reinforces my point. It was this morning, a little over twelve hours ago. Regardless of your instincts or whatever it is that makes you so…comfortable around me, you need to stop. It could kill your career."

She stared at him in wonder. "Aidan, I can't believe after everything you've been through that you're worried about my career. I'm astonished, actually."

"O'Brien."

"What?"

"Don't call me Aidan."

Her fact heated again. "Of course not," she snapped. "Thank you for the reminder."

"Don't look at me like that."

"Like what?"

"Like you're a puppy and I just kicked you. You're not the only one around here feeling a little too comfortable."

Her eyes widened. "Oh. Well, um, then…all I can say is that you sure hide it well."

He stared at her. "Do I?" Ever so slowly, he lifted his hand and gently traced the contour of her cheek.

His touch sent a shock wave through her senses, making her long for so much more. She leaned into his touch—

He jerked his hand back and swore. "I'm trying to warn you and here I am doing the same thing." He shoved both his hands through his hair, leaving it rumpled and disheveled.

Grace's fingers curled with the desire to feather her hands where his had been, to smooth the waves in his hair, to draw him close.

"Stop it," he bit out. "Don't look at me like that, either."

"Like a wounded puppy?"

"Like a damn temptress. You're dangerous. We're dangerous. This has to stop, this…whatever's happening between us. I don't understand it and I sure as hell don't welcome it. Stop being nice and touching me and calling me Aidan with that sexy voice of yours. Nothing good can come of it so just…stop."

He scrubbed the light stubble on his chin. "For the love of… How did we go off on this tangent? That's not what I… The reason I asked about your plans is that I'm worried about your safety, your physical safety. Don't assume that because you were able to put Collier in his place tonight that you'll have the same success against another man who's larger and stronger than you, especially if he catches you off guard."

"Are you trying to scare me into thinking you might hurt me if I'm not careful?"

"Oh, I'd hurt you. No question. By getting you fired as an FBI agent if we aren't careful. But physically? No way. I'd never be violent toward you or any other woman. Under no circumstances could I ever do that."

She stared at him, searching for the truth in his eyes. "You'd never hurt a woman physically. Are you saying that you didn't hurt Elly?"

"What? That's not what I…" He swore again. "This isn't going the way I… Hell. Malone, just be careful, all right? Don't go around stirring up trouble, trying to find the shooter on your own. Take one of the police officers with you."

She started to cross her arms, but the soreness in her bandaged left arm had her straightening instead. "As you've repeatedly pointed out, I'm a federal agent. Before that, I was a police officer. Notice that I'm in town without a partner. My boss trusts me to take care of myself. You should, too."

"Does your boss know that your first day in Mystic Lake has ended with two attempts on your life? And an injury from one of them?"

Her face heated. "That's none of your business."

His jaw worked. "You're right. It's not. But for some reason, when it comes to you, I can't just look the other way. Don't risk your life by heading out alone anywhere. Please. You've been lucky the first two times this guy shot at you, lucky that you're still alive and only have a sore arm and a few stitches out of it. Don't assume he won't make another attempt, and that this time he won't hit something vital."

His impassioned plea, the concern in his expression, had her more confused than ever. Even though she knew he was right that she needed to be careful how she acted around him in front of others, how was she supposed to act in private? She was so convinced he was innocent. Was this sizzling attraction between them completely clouding her judgment? Could he really be guilty of killing the woman he'd claimed to love? The mother of his child?

"Be careful," he repeated, his voice gruff. "Please." He crossed to his room and went inside.

She stood outside her own room, her mind a whirlwind as she considered everything that he'd done or said today. He was hiding something, had to be. Was it about the letters? Had their earlier discussion about them made him think of a possible suspect as their shooter? If so, why not tell her? Because he wanted to handle the situation on his own?

She was just about to go into her room when the rich brogue of Aidan's voice sounded from the other side of his door. He must be on the phone. Who would he call this late at night? Did it have something to do with the case?

Looking around to make sure no one else was in the hallway and that the stairs were empty, she quietly crossed to his door and put her ear against it. Either he was being careful not to be very loud, or the walls in the B and B were insulated really well. She could only make out a few words and phrases.

"Yeah, I know it's late but—"

"Tomorrow. Can't wait for—"

"—what I pay you for."

And finally a name. *"Barnes."*

After that, there was only silence. Fearing she'd made a sound and he was coming to the door to check on it, she hurried across the hall and eased her door shut behind her.

Then she crossed to the bed and took her laptop out of her satchel.

When it was fired up she put two names into the internet search bar. Aidan O'Brien, and Barnes. She tapped Enter, then gasped at the huge amount of search results on her screen. They were mostly news reports about Elly's death, Aidan's arrest, his pleading guilty without a trial. The name Barnes showed up over and over, Nathanial Barnes.

Aidan's defense attorney.

Chapter Ten

Grace adjusted her leather satchel on her shoulder, careful not to hit her sore arm as she headed downstairs the next morning. Her steps were slow both because of her arm and because she was dreading running into Aidan again.

She'd barely slept last night going over everything that had happened and all she'd learned since coming to Mystic Lake. She'd read and reread his folder, searching for inconsistencies, proof about his guilt. Or innocence. But no sooner would she find the answer to one question than she came up with another one. She was more confused than ever.

As soon as she passed the main desk and entered the restaurant, she stopped in surprise. A large group of men and women stood around two long tables that had been pulled end-to-end on the far side of the room. The wording across the backs of their jackets read Polk County Sheriff's Office. They must have arranged for the search party to meet at the restaurant, rather than the station. Seeing how many people were here, it made sense. They'd never have fit in the conference room.

As she headed their way, she saw Chief Dawson bending over the tables, running his fingers across a large map. Beside him were Ortiz and Fletcher. Collier must have been left at the station to run things and take any emergency calls.

"Morning," a familiar brogue said behind her.

She slowly turned around. "Aid—I mean, O'Brien. Morning. Looks like they decided to use this place as their base of operations today."

He nodded in silent approval at her use of his last name. "This is where the town meets for most large gatherings. They say it's for the space. I think it's more about the good food they serve."

"Thanks, Aidan." A smiling Stella had just stepped out of the kitchen with a huge tray of piping-hot blueberry muffins. Grace realized that Stella was the first person she'd heard in this town, other than herself, who'd referred to him by his first name. Did that mean they were friends?

"I won't tell Frank you complimented his cooking," Stella continued. "His ego is too inflated as it is. Morning, Special Agent Malone. Grab a muffin before those deputies pounce on this second batch. You'd think they were starving the way they inhale their food."

"Thank you, ma'am. Looks delicious." Grace took one of the napkins on the tray and picked up a muffin. Her mouth was watering at the aroma. "They smell incredible."

"That's because they are, dear." She winked and offered Aidan a muffin. Instead, he took the tray from her.

"I'll carry it for you," he said.

She put a hand on his shoulder. "That's not necessary. Everyone over there is in law enforcement. I know you're not comfortable around them." She winked at Grace. "Present FBI agent company excluded, of course. You two are obviously friendly. I heard you're both staying together."

Grace almost choked on the bite of muffin she'd just

taken. She hurriedly swallowed and cleared her throat. "Um, no, ma'am. I gave up one of the rooms I…" She stopped when she saw the laughter sparkling in Stella's eyes.

Aidan looked mildly alarmed. "Are you teasing us, ma'am?"

Stella only laughed and reached for the tray of muffins.

Aidan shook his head. "I've got it. I have to work with the deputies and police today anyway. I'm helping them search for the guy who shot the boat yesterday with an arrow."

"Oh my. Well, do be careful. And don't let those outsiders push you around." With that, she headed back into the kitchen.

Grace followed Aidan to the other side of the large room. Conversation died as soon as he slid the tray onto the table. Not because everyone was reaching for food, but because Aidan's reputation obviously preceded him. Just as Stella apparently feared, the deputies moved away from him, acting as if he wasn't worthy to breathe their air.

Anger had her face heating. She started to say something, but Aidan bumped her shoulder. When she looked up, he subtly shook his head.

She realized that Dawson was watching her, too. She nodded in greeting and kept her silence.

Dawson returned his attention to the map. "Let's assign out the grids we just reviewed. You'll work in teams of two. Check in with your team leader every half hour. And don't assume your Kevlar vests will completely stop an arrow. Sometimes they don't. It all depends on the speed of the arrow, the distance it travels, the angle of the hit, any number of factors. I'm no expert on bows and arrows. But I know about Kevlar and spent over an hour last night researching the kinds of vests Polk County uses and my team uses. So trust me when I tell you not to take your safety for granted today. The guy we're dealing with is extremely dangerous and has already proven that he's willing to target law enforcement."

Grace took that as her cue to step away from the group. She didn't want Dawson to point to her as his warning to the others to be more careful. She still needed to report to her boss about her injury and wasn't looking forward to it. Having him hear through the law enforcement grapevine that an FBI officer was shot with an arrow in Mystic Lake wouldn't do her any favors. She needed to call him first thing when she got to the police station.

Fletcher, who'd been standing near Dawson a moment ago, caught up to Grace near the front desk. "Hey, Malone. The chief assigned me to work with you today, if you need me. Did you want to do knock-and-talks?"

"I'd like to. The first people I want to speak to are the ones who were at the festival, especially any witnesses to the shooting. That includes the family who took that picture of…of O'Brien. And the men on the boat, of course."

"I took statements from them yesterday, so I can give you those. If you want to talk to them again, I'll set it up."

"Perfect. I want a tour of the town, as well. In particular, I'm interested in places where a stranger may hide in plain sight without causing suspicion. On the internet I saw there's a large campground near the marina. Or, at least, there used to be. Is that still there? And open this time of year?"

"Colby opened it for the leaf peepers just this week. Colby Wainright, the owner. The first official picture-taking tourists are scheduled to stay at the campground this weekend." She grinned. "I was up early and already called over there."

"Well, there's nothing for me to do, then."

Fletcher laughed. "There's plenty. But I'd like to think I can be helpful in your investigation."

"*Our* investigation. The guy we're after is either a serial killer or a copycat. Either way, we need to stop him to keep everyone safe. I not only appreciate your help, I need it. And I have to add that I've never had such a welcome reception by a non-federal law enforcement agency before. Or even just the locals. Everyone I've met so far, like Stella, the front desk clerk, the few customers who were in the restaurant late last night when I came down for a quick snack, they've all been so friendly. I don't know how Mystic Lake got a reputation for being so, well—"

"Wacky? Weird? Mysterious?"

She laughed. "All of the above, I suppose."

Fletcher rapped her knuckles on the front desk. "That's me knocking on wood, hoping none of our mysterious stuff happens while you're here to ruin your current impression of our town. I kind of like the idea of us being known for being nice instead of our usual rep. Are you ready to head over now? My Jeep's parked out front. I got a prime parking space. Didn't have to drive around back or double-park." She frowned at Grace. "Actually, you might need a heavier jacket today if you plan on canvassing the town, interviewing people. It's chillier this morning than it was yesterday. And it'll be at least ten degrees colder up in the higher elevations."

"Noted. I'll hurry upstairs and be right back."

"I'll get the heater going in the Jeep. Meet you outside."

Once Grace entered her room, she grabbed some napkins from the coffee area to wrap up her barely eaten blueberry muffin to finish at the station. The one bite she'd had was amazing and she was looking forward to finishing it.

Once she had her heavier jacket on, she couldn't resist peeking into the restaurant one more time to see how things were going. To her surprise, Aidan was the one speaking to the group now. He was pointing at the map and she could just hear enough to realize he was warning them about specific areas on his property that had dangerous drop-offs or were perfect locations for an ambush.

Dawson spoke up then, telling them that he'd slipped and started to fall over one of those cliffs yesterday and that Aidan had quite literally risked his own life to save him. Grace could have hugged the chief for admitting that. He clearly knew something needed to be done to change the atmosphere of the team if the search was going to be successful. Sure enough, some of the deputies were looking at Aidan with far less suspicion now, even respect.

As Dawson answered a question from one of the men, Aidan glanced up and met Grace's gaze. He quickly looked away. She sighed and hurried outside to meet Fletcher.

DISAPPOINTMENT SETTLED OVER Aidan as Grace left the restaurant. While he was glad that she was being more careful about how she acted around him, he'd hoped to at least have a couple of minutes to speak to her. He wanted to know where she was going and remind her to have someone with her for safety. And if he could somehow *accidentally* show up where she was later today and check on her, he could at least reassure himself that she was okay. Instead, he'd probably be worrying about her all day not knowing her plans.

He sighed in frustration. What an idiot he was to have

his thoughts so consumed with her. He needed to take his own advice and be careful. The man trying to frame him was likely on the hunt for him. And if that meant he was waiting up on Aidan's property, there was likely an arrow with his name written on it. The only way Aidan was going to survive was to stay alert and focused. Somehow he had to stop thinking about the beautiful, smart, delightfully sassy woman who'd somehow managed to crack the wall around his heart that he'd spent the past twelve years erecting.

"O'Brien." Ortiz motioned to him. "Let's get you fitted in a vest since you're going up with us. It's not a hundred percent protection but it could save your life if you do get hit."

"What about Malone and your officers who aren't participating in the search? If this guy has left the mountain and ends up somewhere they go today, they could be in danger, too.

"Good point. I'll talk to the chief."

Chapter Eleven

Grace followed Fletcher into the police station and was met by Collier wearing a Kevlar vest and holding up two more. "Chief's orders, ladies."

Fletcher settled her hands on her hips. "You're making that up. I've been here two years and have never had to dust one of those off."

"We've never had someone running around town shooting at people with a bow and arrow before, either. Until he's caught, we've been ordered to wear these while on duty."

"Even if we're in the office?" Fletcher complained.

"Even if." He held one out to her.

She grumbled and took it.

"Malone?" He offered her the other one. "Obviously the chief can't force you to wear this. But he highly recommends it. There are a few more in the supply closet if this one doesn't fit."

"Does O'Brien have one? He's with that search party heading up to his place. If anyone should have one it's him since the shooter obviously has a vendetta against him. He might as well have a target on his back."

He grinned. "Funny you should say that. He's the one who asked the chief to make sure you have a vest. And the rest of us, of course." He cocked his head as if considering. "Should we read anything into that?"

Grace rolled her eyes, but her face flushed with heat.

"Leave her alone," Fletcher scolded. "You need any help with those straps, Malone?"

"I think I can manage." She slid it on and began adjusting the Velcro. "This vest is bulkier than the one I normally wear. I may exchange it for mine the next time I'm in my car."

Fletcher motioned toward the conference room. "Did you want to set up in there or use Ortiz's desk? It's not as bad as usual. No crumbs this morning." She chuckled.

Grace smiled and glanced at the proximity of his desk to Fletcher's and Collier's. The angle meant they'd see everything she was doing on her computer, which wasn't necessarily a bad thing. But they'd also hear her on the phone—like when she called her boss to tell him about the fiasco yesterday.

"It *would* be easier to spread everything out in there," Grace said.

"Sounds good. Supplies are in that cabinet by the vending machines if you need anything. For lunch we often have a sandwich shop farther down Main Street deliver. Let me know when you're hungry."

"I appreciate it." Grace headed into the conference room and set her satchel on the table. No sooner had she unloaded her laptop and folders than Collier knocked on the glass door and headed inside. She groaned when she saw he was carrying his medical bag.

"Warned you yesterday that I'd need to check your stitches today and change that bandage. I'm still going to help you, even though you crushed my ego by flipping me over your shoulder. I still don't see how you did that with a hurt arm, especially as small as you are."

"Training. Want me to show you?"

"I'd rather not."

She laughed and sat beside him so he could work on her arm.

"Looks good," he said after he cut the bandage off. "No sign of infection. I'll put some antibiotic ointment on it again and wrap it back up." He set a bottle of pain pills on the table. "Take two of these and call me in the morning." He winked and smeared the ointment on her arm, then expertly re-bandaged it.

"Thanks. Seriously. It feels much better this morning. You did a great job."

"I'm a jack of all trades. Part-time doctor—"

"EMT."

"—full-time police officer who looks great in a uniform. Good-looking and single. Know anyone who might appreciate that?" He waggled his brows at her.

"Are you flirting with me, Officer Collier?"

"You can call me Chris."

"I'd rather not."

He dramatically pressed his hand against his chest. "My hopes are dashed."

The door opened and Fletcher stood in the opening. "Collier, leave the pretty FBI agent alone. I see what you're doing. The walls are glass. Plus, I know *you*."

"I was taking care of my patient."

"Asking her out on a date, more likely. Ignore whatever he said to you, Malone. He flirts with any woman who will talk to him. It's just what he does. He's actually harmless."

"Don't forget good-looking." He sighed at Malone. "Maybe next time."

Malone couldn't help laughing at his antics.

Fletcher grabbed his arm and pulled him out of the room, lecturing him on professionalism the whole time.

It was obvious that they were good friends in addition to being coworkers. Like a brother and sister, their good-natured teasing and nagging spoke of a strong bond beneath the surface. She'd sensed that same camaraderie from the whole team when they'd all been together. Grace couldn't help the tug of jealousy inside her.

She didn't have any close friends at work. The stress and high expectations and constant evaluations during her training hadn't allowed the time or casualness that would enable friendships to develop. Maybe once this investigation was over, if she did a good job, that would change. She'd love to experience the closeness the police here at Mystic Lake shared.

Grace started separating out her various reports and photographs, getting them organized so she could plan her next steps. Once everything was set, she logged on to the FBI portal to see whether the lab report was back on the first batch of evidence she'd had couriered yesterday. So far there was nothing. Unable to justify delaying any longer, she did the thing she'd been dreading most. She called her boss.

It didn't go well.

He was ticked about her being injured and wanted her to go home, immediately. He'd send another agent to look into what had happened to confirm or disprove her suspicions that the shooter they were dealing with wasn't the serial killer they were after.

She in turn appealed to his love of efficiency by arguing that the more experienced agents should use their skills
to their best advantage by continuing to follow up on the
leads from the Crossbow Killer's known crime scenes. It
made far more sense to leave the junior agent following
up on a lead they doubted would pan out. Besides, she had
the entire police force of Mystic Lake backing her up, plus
a dozen deputies from Polk County. The odds of anything
else bad happening to her were almost zero.

What she'd said wasn't an outright lie. But she knew he'd
assume the police force was more than four people. And
he didn't realize the deputies were here only for today to
assist with a search. Luckily, he didn't dive deeper into the
logistics. But he didn't agree to let her stay, either. Instead,
he gave her twenty-four hours to report back on her progress, and her health. Once she called tomorrow morning
with an update, he'd make a final decision about her continuing role in Mystic Lake.

She blew out a shaky breath and ended the call. Assuming today's search didn't result in the arrest of a suspect,
she needed to show solid progress and not get into trouble
again. Those knock-and-talks had just become critical. But
before she headed out to conduct interviews, she wanted to
read the ones that Fletcher had already conducted.

Fletcher had been extremely thorough. Grace couldn't
find any fault with her work. She'd asked all of the questions Grace would have, and then some. Her knowledge of
both the town and its people was obviously a great asset.
It gave her the background to know what types of things
to ask about, specific to each person interviewed, things
that wouldn't have occurred to Grace.

She secured her laptop to the metal ring in the tabletop

using a cable lock. Then she grabbed a small notepad and pen and slid them into her jacket pocket as she exited the conference room.

Collier was on the phone, taking notes, and nodded at her, preoccupied with whatever he was working on.

Fletcher looked up from her desktop computer, her glance falling to Grace's jacket. "Are we going somewhere?"

"If your offer to help me with interviews is still open, yes. I was impressed with the ones you did yesterday. I'd appreciate your assistance today."

The officer's face lit up with pleasure. "Lo and behold, I impressed a Fed. I'll bet Collier can't say the same." When he didn't even look her way, she rolled her eyes. "It's no fun teasing him if he isn't paying attention." She grabbed her jacket and shrugged it on over her vest, frowning and readjusting the straps before zipping her jacket. "Did you have any specific place in mind where you want to start?"

"The campground."

Chapter Twelve

Aidan dropped to his knees on the ground and peered over the edge of the cliff. Relief swept through him when he saw Ortiz standing on the rock overhang below, clinging to a sapling growing out of the side of the mountain. Another foot and he'd have tumbled down to the ravine.

"Did I or did I not tell you to stop?" Aidan laughed when Ortiz made a rude gesture.

"I tried to, but the dang rocks were like ice, sliding out from under me. Whatever you paid for this piece of property, you paid too much," Ortiz complained. "It's a nightmare of cliffs and rock and vegetation so thick you can hardly see twenty feet in front of you."

"The cabin and flat land around it are nice enough to make up for that. And it's the views I paid for, and great hunting. Those rocks and cliffs you're complaining about are a bonus. They make it secure and hard for people to trespass. Well, usually, anyway."

"Maybe the shooter decided the same thing and went somewhere else. Or better yet, maybe he's at the bottom of one of these ravines and we'll find his skeleton after the buzzards pick it clean. You gonna haul me up, or talk me to death?"

"I was thinking of taking a picture first to show Dawson when we rendezvous with the rest of the search party."

Ortiz swore and tried to climb up the cliff wall on his own.

"Stop, stop," Aidan said, laughing. "Give me a minute. I need leverage." He looked around, then chose two trees close to the edge to brace his legs. After taking off his belt, he made a loop, then held it down toward Ortiz. "Loop your belt through mine and around your wrists. Then use your legs to push against the rock and climb up while I pull."

Ortiz did as he'd said, then warned, "If you drop me, I'm going to come back and haunt you."

"Would you rather I call your boss and have him pull you up?"

"Hell, no. If you even hint that I needed rescuing, I'll swear you're lying."

Aidan snorted and pulled the belt tight. "Let's do this."

A minute later, they were both lying on their backs above the drop-off, trying to catch their breath.

"That was fun," Ortiz said between taking gulps of air. "Particularly the part where you said uh-oh as if you were going to drop me."

Aidan sat up. "Consider it karma, payback for handcuffing me to the conference room table. It's nice having law enforcement at my mercy for a change instead of the other way around."

Ortiz grunted and sat up, too, taking his belt from Aidan. Once they were both standing and well away from the edge, Aidan motioned toward a slight incline on their right. "That's the last part of our grid to search. This time, stay beside or behind me. Don't get impatient and speed ahead. Slow and steady means staying safe."

"I get it. Trust me, I get it." A moment later he called out, "O'Brien? Aidan? Wait."

Aidan turned in question.

Ortiz seemed uncomfortable, looking off in the distance before finally dragging in a deep breath. "I, uh, I don't pretend to know much about what happened in your past, the reasons behind what you did and exactly what took place." He held up his hands. "And I'm not asking you to explain. It's just, I may have misjudged you this past year. I lumped you in with all the other, well, criminals I've known through the years and assumed you were as bad as, or worse than, them. But none of those others would have done what you've done. I—"

"Forget it," Aidan said. "You probably could have climbed up that drop-off without my help. It just would have taken longer."

"That's not what I'm talking about. I mean, yeah, maybe I could have. But then again, maybe I would have fallen." He grimaced. "I appreciate your help, and that you helped the chief when he had a close call. And a lot of other things, like you running into the woods at the festival to try to get the shooter, with no thought for your own safety."

"Ortiz, we need to finish searching our grid and—"

"Just give me a second, man. I'm eating crow here. Let me finish."

Aidan sighed. "The sun will set soon. Let's search while you eat crow."

Ortiz followed him up the incline. "I'm just saying there's more to you than your past. Not that what you did was okay or anything. But I honestly believe people can change. And the man I've seen these past couple of days isn't the man I always thought you were."

Aidan stopped and pushed some small branches aside to peer underneath a bush.

"I'll try to give you the benefit of the doubt from now on," Ortiz said, stopping beside him. "And I'll make an effort to not always assume you're behind every little bad thing that happens around here. That's what I'm trying to say."

Aidan pointed beneath the bush. "Is that what I think it is?"

Ortiz leaned down to look at the plastic bag Aidan had found. "Well, I'll be. Look at all these feathers. At least now we know where they came from. It isn't his hunting prowess, unless you call going to a costume store hunting. I wonder if that shopping bag has a receipt in it. Or fingerprints." He pulled some latex gloves out of his pocket and pulled them on. "No receipt, but I recognize the bag. Comes from a party store in town. Not Mystic Lake—Chattanooga. I take my daughter there to shop for Halloween every year."

"The paint on the feathers looks fresh." Aidan bent down to check for a discarded paint can or brush, but didn't find any.

"Why would he leave the feathers behind after going to all that trouble?" Ortiz asked.

Aidan glanced back in the direction of the cliff that Ortiz had slid down. It wasn't far, maybe twenty yards. He located shoe prints near the bush, then backtracked, following them to see where else the shooter had been.

When he and Ortiz reached the cliff's edge, the officer's face went pale.

"He was here," Ortiz said. "He was standing right here, maybe trying to see where all the searchers were."

Aidan nodded. "He must have heard us coming and ran and hid in those bushes. That bag crinkles, makes noise.

Most likely he ditched it because he was worried we'd hear him. He must not have had his bow and arrows with him or he'd have shot at us."

"Lord have mercy," Ortiz said, his face still pale.

"He's on the run. I doubt he's gotten very far. This is the most treacherous terrain on my property. It's slow going. There are only two ways out: the way we came, or off to the left over there, northeast."

Ortiz pulled out his cell phone. "I'll warn the others."

Chapter Thirteen

The sun was beginning to set before Fletcher and Grace completed most of the interviews that Grace felt were necessary for her investigation. There were a few more they'd do tomorrow. She just hoped the work she'd done today was sufficient for her boss to allow her to continue. Investigations took time and at least she was making progress. And, bonus, there hadn't been another attempt on her life. So far.

The campground had been a bust: no new leads. But it covered several acres and it took a long time to thoroughly search the surrounding woods for signs that someone may have been staying there, hiding out. They didn't even find a cigarette butt or a beer can to indicate anyone had been there. Then again, since the owner, Colby, was in the process of getting it ready for his first reservations of the season, he'd been cleaning daily. So there was no real way to know if he'd thrown away what could have been evidence.

He didn't remember seeing anyone suspicious but admitted there were always a few hikers or walkers in the area and he didn't pay them much attention. He maintained a network of trails for his campers. The locals used them as well, which he appreciated because it kept the vegetation from taking over. But, no, he hadn't seen any strangers, or at least, he didn't remember any.

Although Grace and Fletcher had spoken to just about everyone Fletcher could think of who'd attended the festival, which was actually easy since so many of them were regulars at Stella's restaurant, none of the people they'd spoken to remembered seeing any strangers.

As Fletcher's Jeep bumped around the back roads on their return to the police station, she apologized that they hadn't accomplished anything.

"Sure we did," Grace said. "We spoke to almost everyone we needed to talk to. That's progress."

"I don't see how. We didn't learn anything."

"We learned quite a bit. Think about it. Everyone we spoke to said the same thing, that they didn't notice any strangers around. What does that tell you?"

Fletcher steered around a tree that was blocking half the gravel road they were heading down. "I'll have to call that in, get someone up here to clear it. Um, let's see. What does that tell me. I guess just that no one saw our guy. Maybe he's a ghost, one of those poltergeists who can move things. It would fit in with other alleged spiritual sightings in the area."

"Fletcher—"

"I know, I know. No one saw him even though we know he exists, poltergeists excluded. Like I said, we made no progress."

"We know he's around, has been for a few days at least. If no one saw a *stranger*, then our shooter is…"

"I don't know, he's…wait. A local. That's what you're saying?"

"It's a possibility."

"No way. Can't be. There's no one in this town that I can picture shooting at people with a bow and arrow. Not even the rottenest of the teenage menaces who like to have bonfires in the woods without caring that they could set the whole forest on fire would go around shooting arrows at people. It can't be a local."

"Let's add those teenage menaces to the list for additional interviews. I'm not ready to discount that our suspect could be a local. But let's say you're right and he isn't. What does that leave us with, remembering that no one has noticed anyone unfamiliar to them in town?"

Fletcher thought for a moment, then shrugged. "No idea. What's your theory?"

"It's more like a building block than a theory, something to start giving us a more clear idea, or profile, of the person we're after. If he's a stranger, not a local, then to not have been seen around town means he's not going to the restaurants or shops. He's not staying at the campground and not stealing a boat or canoe from the marina since they didn't report any missing. He's likely not broken into anyone's homes or vacation cabins looking for food or shelter or you'd have had someone reporting that."

"Oh, I get what you're saying. He's comfortable with the outdoors. He's self-reliant, used to camping in the wilderness, on his own, away from everyone else. He's avoiding the town and the people in it, except for when he wants to strike, like at the festival or at O'Brien's place. Most likely he has a tent, a sleeping bag, provisions. When he came here he came prepared with all the supplies he'd need to survive until he accomplished whatever he came here to do."

Grace grimaced. "To get revenge against O'Brien for something. Framing him didn't work, so his next step may well be to try to kill him. But go back to what you just said. You mentioned when he came here. How did he get here? There's only one road in and out. I suppose the river is an option."

"No, it's not. It feeds our lake, but if you trace it up the mountain you'll see a giant waterfall, Mystic Falls. It's one of our tourist attractions around here, especially in the spring when it swells from the winter thaw. It's pretty incredible, but it's in no way navigable. Even a boat or canoe would be busted up on the rocks if someone tried to navigate the river over the falls. The only way to get a boat here is on a trailer behind your vehicle. Most people just rent a boat already at the marina rather than go to that kind of trouble."

Grace considered what she'd said and looked up at the steep, treacherous mountain Fletcher was carefully descending to get them back to town. "I suppose, in theory, someone determined enough could hike in over the mountains, couldn't they?"

"Ha. Not likely. You've seen how unforgiving the land is around O'Brien's place. We've got spots like that all around here. Makes it darn near impossible to approach our town that way. It's one of the reasons our town stays small, even with the attractions for tourists. To move here, you have to either buy someone out or have the money to dynamite and excavate a part of the mountain to make it possible to build on in the first place. We're truly landlocked. One way in, one way out."

"The road through the mountains and forest to reach Mystic Lake is an hour by car," Grace said. "How long would it take to walk that distance?"

"Me? About a week." She laughed. "Okay, maybe not

that long. But you drove here, you saw how the road winds around the mountains, constantly going up and down. It would be a challenge to anyone to do that without a vehicle. Even one of those iron man athletes would struggle. No, I think he drove here."

"All right, then how hard would it be to hide a vehicle once you arrive so that no one reports seeing it?"

"I like where you're going with that," Fletcher said. "Collier, to his credit, is an explorer at heart. His idea of a vacation is to hike the mountains around our town. I think that's crazy. I'd rather go to some nice warm beach and work on a tan. But my point is that he knows the land that surrounds our town better than most. We can put him on that, have him map out the area and figure out the places where someone might likely hide their vehicle so we can check them out. Who knows, maybe we'll get lucky and catch our suspect napping in his back seat or the bed of his pickup."

"There's something else we could do," Grace added. "With only three officers, I know you can't spare someone to keep an eye on the road out of town 24/7. But maybe a camera could be set up to record the license plates of anyone leaving the area. We can check those out in case our suspect leaves. That would be like a gift from heaven, having a plate to track. Unless of course his vehicle is stolen. But even that would give us another clue. Maybe he stole it in an area where he's most comfortable. You never know what that might lead to."

Fletcher stopped at the very road they were discussing, checked for cars, then turned in the direction of Mystic Lake. "I think a camera on this road is a perfect idea. We can borrow a trail camera from one of our local hunters, the kind that's activated by motion so the battery doesn't run out right away. One of us can change out the video card every day and bring the used one back to the station to check out on our computer."

"About how many vehicles head out of town every day?"

"More than I'd like when it comes to figuring out which cars belong to people who live here and which ones don't. Since the pandemic changed how people do business, a lot more of our town telecommutes, works from home. But there are still quite a few who have to drive to Chattanooga every day. Don't worry, though. We'll track everything down, see if there's a lone, unexplained vehicle coming in or out of town."

Grace was happy to have a plan, even if just one to try to get a license plate and vehicle description that may or may not help them find the killer. That was the thing about investigative leads. You could never predict which one would pan out, so you had to follow up on all of them.

"You haven't heard any updates about today's search, right?" she asked.

"Not a peep. But I'm sure everyone's okay or we definitely would have been called. Most likely the deputies are either on their way back to Chattanooga or are there already. No one's going to search up here at night, especially on O'Brien's property. That's some of the roughest terrain I've seen anyone living on around here. It's downright dangerous."

"Which means our suspect is even more comfortable and knowledgeable about the outdoors than your typical hunter or even camper would be. He was able to get away from your boss and O'Brien when he shot at me." She grimaced. "*Both times* he shot at me. A novice outdoorsman wouldn't have been able to get away, not without getting hurt or cornered. He's highly skilled."

Fletcher snorted. "Except for that stupid feather thing on the end of his arrows. He'd have way better aim if he didn't use that. He must not know much about using a bow and arrow or he'd ditch the feathers."

Grace stared at her a moment. "You may be right. O'Brien theorized that the shooter doesn't care who he hits. The victim is random. They just happen to be in the way of wherever the arrow lands. Honestly, that makes the most sense for our profile since our other evidence points to this guy being an experienced outdoorsman. He knows the feather throws off his aim and he doesn't care. It's because he's bragging. He wants everyone to know that he's the one hurting or killing people. The feather is his signature."

"You're talking about this Crossbow Killer again. I thought you were thinking our shooter probably wasn't him, that he was someone specifically after O'Brien."

"I can't discount the possibility that the real serial killer could also be after O'Brien for some reason. It seems unlikely. Doesn't fit in with typical serial killer behavior, if you can call any of their behavior typical. But we don't have enough information to arrive at a conclusion about that. As for the picture of our shooter that we're trying to draw, I think we *can* conclude that he's in good physical condition or he wouldn't be able to run through the woods in rough terrain to escape the police. That means he's young, but old enough that he's likely had years of experience in the wilderness. I'd say mid- to late twenties, maybe even early thirties."

"Honestly, I'm leaning more toward those teenage locals again," Fletcher said. "Kids around here start hunting and hiking and practically living outdoors from a really young age. They can be experts outdoors before they even graduate. I'll draw up a list of our frequent offenders. And I can ask the school principal if there's anyone else he thinks we should consider, maybe someone who's a loner or even a bully, something like that."

"I wouldn't have thought Mystic Lake was large enough to have any schools. Or do the kids commute to Chattanooga?"

Fletcher laughed. "Believe it or not, we have enough residents to support a K-through-twelve school and a one-truck fire station in addition to our little police force. You don't see everyone because the town's population is spread out over a vast area, all up and down the mountains. There's even a subdivision past the marina. We ran out of time today to go that far. But we really have a lot to offer for just about anyone, whether you want to live in the mountains or the burbs." She rolled her eyes. "Listen to me. I should be on the town council heading up the tourism task force."

"You do make Mystic Lake sound pretty nice."

"Except for our resident serial killer or copycat?"

Grace laughed. "Except for that."

They were close to where the woods ended and the town began. Grace tapped her hand impatiently on her thigh. "I hope the lab gets back to me soon. I really need to know what they've found, whether the evidence we sent matches the evidence from our previous crime scenes. It will help us cull all these theories and ideas of ours if we know whether we're looking for the Crossbow Killer or someone else entirely."

Fletcher turned onto Main Street, then slowed to a stop. "What the ever loving...the dang media's here. Look at that news truck parked a few spots down from the station. They wouldn't have driven all this way for a story about a random arrow shot during our festival, especially since no one was hurt. And, honestly, that's not exactly unusual around here compared to other things that go on. I'm betting one of those Polk County deputies sprang a leak. He probably has a friend at the news desk and told them we were searching for a potential serial killer out here."

She glanced at Grace. "Seeing an FBI agent, or even knowing you're here if the deputies shared that information, too, is going to make the reporter rabid. It could spread like a disease and we'll have even more of them here tomorrow. Let's enter the station through the back door. There's a service alley behind all the shops we can use."

She parked on the far side of the main parking lot. As soon as the two of them sneaked into the station, Collier looked up with a relieved expression on his face. "I was just about to call you two and warn you that—"

"The news media's outside," Fletcher interrupted. "We saw the van."

"A cameraman and reporter got here about fifteen minutes ago demanding to see the chief about the search being done for a serial killer. I did what I could to laugh that off and said we were actually after some kid playing pranks. They asked me if that was the case why was there an FBI agent in town. I told them we take the security of our citizens very seriously and when the kid almost hurt someone at the festival we called in the FBI to help us nip this thing as quickly as possible. But as you can see, they're still here. I don't think they believed anything I told them."

Grace groaned. "My boss will love this. He wanted to keep everything quiet until I determined if our killer is really here or not. Does Dawson know the media is waiting to pounce on him?"

"I warned him right before you came in. He should be here soon. They called the search off half an hour ago and the deputies are on their way back home."

"Good riddance," Fletcher said as she hung her jacket on the back of her chair.

"Agreed. They did find signs of our suspect and that he was there recently. But he's a slippery devil. No one actually saw him in spite of all those searchers. Justin's scent dog pulled up lame, so he wasn't any help today or they might have had better luck."

"What kinds of signs did they find?" Grace asked. "Is there more evidence for our lab to process?"

The squeak of the back door followed by footsteps had all of them turning. Chief Dawson entered, followed by Ortiz and Aidan.

"Lock the front door," Dawson told Collier. "Quickly, before that reporter notices I'm here. I'm not in the mood to be civil at the moment. The search was a bust."

Collier hurried to lock the door while Ortiz set a large paper evidence bag on his desk.

"Not a total bust," Ortiz said. "We have a plastic bag from a costume store in Chattanooga and half a dozen white feathers, painted with the same red stripe as the earlier ones, ready to be attached to more arrows."

Grace hurried over and looked in the bag while Ortiz held it open. "This is great. I'll arrange for another courier in the morning to get this to the lab. But I'd like to follow up with the store you mentioned. I don't see a name on the bag."

"I'll give you the info," Ortiz said. "That sparkly bag

is unique. Even without a store name on it, I recognized it immediately."

Grace glanced at Aidan. "O'Brien, did everything go well? Any close calls?"

Ortiz shot Aidan a look as if in warning and answered for him. "No close calls. Nothing happened except that we got lucky and found that evidence. Like the chief said, it was a waste of time. I don't know how this guy keeps managing to give us the slip. At this point it's embarrassing."

"Dang right it is," Dawson said. "Which is why I have no interest in speaking to the media. We can deal with them tomorrow. Everyone head home—the back way, of course. If you do get cornered by a reporter the answer is no comment. Understood?"

"Yes, sir," all three officers chimed in at the same time.

Dawson crossed the room toward his office.

"I'll let dispatch know we're transferring the phones to them now," Collier said.

At Grace's questioning look, he explained, "As long as one of us is at the station, we take any emergency calls. When no one is here we transfer emergency calls to a call center, basically the same 911 operators who support the sheriff's office. If there is an emergency call at night, which is rare for us, the operators do what they can to talk the caller through whatever emergency is going on. And, of course, they contact whichever one of us is on point."

Fletcher bumped his shoulder. "Lucky you. You're on call tonight."

He made a face at her.

Dawson came out of his office carrying a small satchel, perhaps paperwork he wanted to take home, and motioned to Grace. "Make sure you keep your jacket covering your vest. You, too, O'Brien, unless you want the reporter to hit you up with questions thinking you're a cop. If everyone's ready to go, we'll head out the back together. As soon as we hit the lights, that reporter is going to realize they've been tricked and I'm not giving them an interview. They'll figure out pretty quickly that there must be a back door. We'll have to hustle if we're going to get in our cars before they find us. O'Brien and Malone, I'll give you a ride to the B and B to run interference, just in case. Hopefully you can get upstairs before being ambushed."

No sooner did the chief drop off Grace and Aidan than the news van pulled up behind his Jeep. Luckily for them, the reporter ran up to the driver's door to talk to Dawson. Grace and Aidan ducked down and hurried into the B and B and upstairs without having to deal with the media.

When they reached the landing at the top of the stairs, Aidan nodded goodbye and turned toward his room.

"Wait," Grace said. "Please."

He hesitated, then faced her with a questioning look.

The sound of voices in the lobby had her glancing toward the stairs. She lowered her voice so no one downstairs would hear. "I really need to talk to you."

"That's not a good idea—"

"It's work-related. I want to brainstorm with you about the shooter."

His jaw tightened. "You mean you want to interrogate me again."

"You're not a suspect. You're the suspect's target. So far, that's the best lead I have to figure out who this guy may be. I'd like to ask you some questions and see if we can come up with any ideas, a new direction for me to take my investigation. Otherwise, I'm stuck waiting on lab results and a search for a vehicle that may or may not exist."

"Vehicle?"

"I'll explain, once we sit down to talk. We could go in one of our rooms and—"

"No."

She put her hands on her hips. "Are you afraid of me, Aidan? Afraid I'm going to jump your bones or something? I'm not that desperate."

He choked on a laugh, then cleared his throat. "My ego just got crushed knowing you'd have to be desperate to want me. But at least I'm safe knowing you won't try to jump my bones."

"As much as you complain, I think you're the one who's worried you can't keep your hands off me if we're in a bedroom together."

Instead of the immediate denial she'd expected in response to her teasing, he simply stared at her. The amber brown of his eyes seemed to get even darker, more intense. There was no sign of amusement or an impending snappy comeback. Instead, he reminded her of a sleek panther, ready to pounce.

An answering hunger flared inside her. When he quickly turned back to his room and unlocked the door, she was there right behind him. He whirled around, his hands clasping her wrists with a solid yet remarkably gentle grip, stopping her.

"Grace, don't. I'm trying to do right by you. But you're not making it easy."

The sound of voices again froze both of them in place.

"Can't say I've ever met a TV reporter before." The sound of Stella's voice in the lobby seemed louder than usual. Her next words had Grace in a panic. "Two nights then. I don't have any more vacancies after that. We're all booked up for the fall season. It's number three, top of the stairs then take a right and it's at the end of the hall."

Footsteps sounded on the stairs, quick and light, heading up.

"Ah, hell." Aidan yanked Grace into his room and shut the door.

Chapter Fourteen

Aidan leaned past Grace and flipped the dead bolt. Then he froze. Without meaning to, he'd pressed her back against the door. There wasn't an inch of space between them. Even with their jackets and vests on he could feel her heat and the pressure of her generous curves crushed against his chest. He should back up, put as much distance as possible between them. But he couldn't have moved away right now if the fires of hell were licking at his heels. She felt so…dang…good.

His body responded against his will, hardening against her. The soft intake of her breath had his pulse rushing in his ears. And then, the impossible happened. This smart, beautiful woman who was too good for him for so many reasons slid her hands up his coat, their heat practically burning him when she stroked the sides of his neck. Standing on tiptoes, she thrust her fingers into his hair where it touched the back of his collar, stroking, kneading, fanning the flames.

He shuddered against her and suddenly they were both stripping each other's jackets off, then their vests, tossing them onto the floor. She plastered her body against his, her mouthwatering curves fitting perfectly against his hard planes.

"Kiss me," she whispered. "Kiss me, Aidan."

His good intentions, his self-control, melted away in the inferno they'd created. He spanned her tiny waist with his hands and lifted her. She wrapped her legs around him and he pressed her against the door, shoving one hand through her hair, the other supporting her bottom as he claimed her mouth with his.

It was as if dynamite had exploded between them, burning away all logic, all reason, every thought in his mind except loving her. He couldn't get enough, stroking, caressing, kissing her the way he'd wanted to from the moment she'd impressed him by knowing what type of wood he was using to make that dang table in his workshop. She was a confusing mix of intelligence and wonder, aggravating him one moment and enthralling him the next. And just when he was about to end their kiss, his lungs starving for air, she deepened it and thrust her delicate tongue inside his mouth.

His legs nearly buckled. He groaned and matched her wild hunger with his own, no longer even trying to hold back. He wanted this, needed this. And he could sense the answering need in her. They were ravenous for each other. Turning with her in his arms, he rushed to the bed, careful not to crush her as he followed her down to the mattress.

He forced himself to slow down, to savor, to be gentle to this beautiful, delicate woman who was so much smaller than him. But as much as he wanted her, he wanted to make this good for her, to show her with his actions how obsessed he was with her even if he couldn't put it into words or had tried to pretend indifference.

"I'm not going to break," she whispered against his neck. "Love me. Just love me. Let yourself go."

Her sexy plea had him groaning again, shaking with need. It had been so long, so dang long.

Twelve years.

He stilled.

It had been twelve years since he'd made love to a woman, the only woman he'd ever been with.

Elly.

Shame washed over him like a bucket of ice water. Not because he was betraying Elly, but because he was thinking of his wife while loving Grace. It was wrong. This was wrong. If he made love to Grace it needed to be in the right setting, the right frame of mind, without a ghost between them. She deserved better. *Grace* deserved better.

"Aidan? What's wrong?"

He swore softly and pressed a kiss against her forehead, before shoving himself to his feet. Leaning down, he gently grasped her hands and pulled her to stand in front of him.

"I'm so sorry, Grace. I just… I can't do this."

Her brow crinkled in confusion and she looked down. "Um, yes, you can. Trust me. You're standing at glorious, rather impressive attention."

He laughed, then groaned. "I *won't* do this. Believe me, I want to. I can't tell you how badly I ache to…but it's not… I can't… Elly—"

She gasped and scrambled away, her cheeks flushing a bright pink. "My name is Grace. Oh my gosh, I can't believe this happened, or almost happened. Were you thinking about her all along, from the moment we touched?"

"What? No, no. You don't understand. It's been a long time and I—"

"I get it, okay?" She grabbed her vest and jacket off the floor. "I really do understand. And I'm not mad or even hurt. It just…startled me. You're still in love with her." She hesitated, then stepped to him and cupped the side of his face, her gaze searching his. "And there's nothing wrong with that. She was your wife, the mother of your child. You lost her in a horrific way and you're not ready to move on." She grimaced. "I admit I'm mildly mortified for throwing myself at you. But I'll survive. I'm a big girl. I'll be okay. We're okay, all right? Just…forget this ever happened."

She hurried to the door and looked through the peep-hole, then glanced back at him. "Maybe you'll be able to heal and move on once I prove your innocence and exonerate you. I promise I won't give up until I find a way to clear your name."

He stared at her in shock. "What? Grace, no. You don't need to—"

"Don't worry. I've got this." She hurried out of his room and quietly closed the door behind her.

Prove his innocence? Exonerate him? This was a night-mare. He adjusted his clothes with a grimace, then strode to the door and flung it open.

Grace had opened her door, but instead of going inside, she stood in the doorway, both hands covering her mouth, her vest and jacket forgotten on the floor where she must have dropped them.

"What is it?" he asked. "Did someone break into your room?" He jogged across the landing, then stopped behind her, his mouth going dry. Framed in the large picture win-dow on the other side of her room was the highest moun-tain in Mystic Lake. And the very top of it was consumed in flickering reds and yellows lighting up the night sky. Flames.

"Aidan," she breathed, "do you know what's up there?"

Dread settled deep in his gut. "There's only one thing at the top of that mountain. My home."

Chapter Fifteen

The anguish Grace felt as she helplessly watched the volunteer firefighters pump water from one of the creeks on Aidan's property onto the inferno that was his cabin was nothing compared to watching Aidan.

He stood a good twenty feet away from Grace and the police, his face stoic as his personal belongings were consumed by the flames, everything except the eight-by-ten picture frame he cradled against his chest. He'd risked his life running inside the cabin when he and Grace arrived and he'd had to be forced outside by firefighters—all to save a picture of his wife and son. It broke Grace's heart seeing him clutch that photograph, knowing he could have died trying to save it.

Everything he owned outside of his business was burning to the ground. Even the workshop on the far side of the cabin had been torched. The smell of some kind of accelerant was heavy in the air. This wasn't an accident. Someone had purposely set Aidan's home on fire. The only question was, did they know he wasn't there? Or had they hoped to trap him inside as they'd doused the logs and lit them up?

Grace coughed, the air smoky and hot. But in spite of that, she longed to get even closer to the fire, because that was where Aidan was standing. She wanted him to know she was there for him, her career be damned. But other than telling the firefighters that no one else lived here and that he didn't have any pets inside, he hadn't even looked her way. But she didn't have to see his eyes to know what she'd see: the same haunted look they'd had when she'd bumped into him on the sidewalk on her first day in Mystic Lake.

This land, this cabin and workshop, had been his fresh start, his chance to rebuild his life after a decade spent in prison. Now it was crumbling to the ground in front of him.

The firefighters shouted a warning. They hurriedly backed away from the structure moments before the upper floor crashed down onto the first floor. Seconds later, the rest of the building caved in. Nothing about the mass of broken, burning logs resembled the majestic cabin that had once stood in their place. All of Aidan's hopes and dreams had just disintegrated.

Did he feel as if nothing he'd done in the past year mattered? Once again he was the felon, the ex-con with no home, nowhere to go. The road ahead must look bleak, an endless stretch of loneliness and emptiness. It broke her heart seeing him this way. There was no magical fix for his pain, nothing she could do but wait and be here if he should turn to her for solace.

"Malone." Dawson moved close to be heard over the crackling roar of the flames. "We're heading down the mountain to wash off this smoke and get a few hours' sleep. We can't work with the fire marshal on the investigation until the fire's out and cold anyway. I recommend you do the same. You'll be as busy as us in the morning trying to see if this is linked to our as-yet-unnamed bow and arrow suspect."

She glanced at Aidan, still staring at the flames that were finally beginning to die down.

"Go ahead without me."

"Malone." He leaned even closer, his voice low, for her ears only. "It won't look good if you stay here with O'Brien. The firefighters will notice. People talk. Don't forget that reporter's in town. She'll be up here as soon as she can sneak around the roadblock our volunteers set up farther down this mountain."

"I'm staying."

He sighed heavily, then motioned to the others.

IF IT HAD been anything but fire, Aidan didn't think it would have bothered him all that much to lose the cabin. It was insured. He was financially sound, easily able to bear the costs of living somewhere else during the process of re-building. But seeing his home engulfed in flames had hit him like a runaway freight train, catapulting him back to that awful night when he'd turned onto his street and had seen the fire engines, the police, his home burning to the ground. The pain of not knowing if his wife and son were alive or dead had ripped him apart. He'd been so relieved and overjoyed to discover that his son was unharmed and being taken care of by a neighbor. But then he'd learned about his wife.

Burned.

Her spine crushed by a falling beam.

Paralyzed.

On a ventilator the rest of her life.

Many months later, a small miracle had him overjoyed and full of hope. Elly had regained enough movement and control in her right hand to try writing. He'd hurried to position a pen between her fingers and set a pad of paper on her lap. For the first time since the fire, she'd finally be able to communicate with him. But his happiness had quickly turned to horror when he'd managed to decipher the painstakingly scrawled words she'd written.

Let me die.

He squeezed his eyes shut, but it didn't erase the image burned into his mind. His vibrant, beautiful young wife wrote that same thing on the pad of paper every day. And later, when he'd gotten her that special valve to allow her to speak, she'd verbalized what she'd been writing.

Let me die.

"Mr. O'Brien? Sir?"

Aidan's eyes flew open. A fireman stood in front of him, his tan-and-yellow jacket blackened with soot.

"Sir, an investigator will be up here later in the day when the rubble is cool enough to allow an inspection. Please don't try to search for any mementos yet. It's too dangerous."

Aidan glanced at the remnants of his life, shocked to see that the fire truly was out. He was equally surprised to realize that he and the firefighters waiting in the truck were the only ones who remained. Everyone else had gone. Just how long had he stared off into space, focused on the past and not even aware of what was going on around him?

"Mr. O'Brien? Did you hear me, sir?"

"Sorry, yes. Is everyone okay? None of your people got hurt fighting the fire, I hope."

The fireman smiled. "Nothing that a hot shower and long nap won't cure. I recommend you do the same. Standing around here breathing in the smoky air isn't good for anyone. Do you have somewhere to stay?"

"I've got a room in town."

"What about food? Money for clothes? We have a victim's fund. It's not much, but it can get you through for a few weeks until insurance kicks in."

Aidan stared at him, shocked at the kindness he was offering when most people crossed to the other side of the street when they saw him coming. "Do you know who I am?"

"If you're asking whether I've heard rumors about your past, yes. I have. I'm not here to judge. I'm here to help. All of us are." He pointed over his shoulder at the firefighters waiting in the truck. "It's why we do what we do. That victim's fund is open to anyone in need. I can give you the information and you can submit an application. Approval in a situation like this is a guarantee. You'll have some funds within a few hours of submitting the application and—"

"I don't need the money. But thank you. I appreciate it. And thank you for keeping the fire from spreading and endangering anyone else."

The other man clasped Aidan's shoulder in sympathy. "I'd ask if you need a ride down the mountain, but it looks like you've got transportation over there. The sooner you get some fresh air, the better. Don't stay up here much longer."

With the fire truck slowly picking its way down the treacherous mountain road, Aidan took one long last look at what remained of the life he'd tried to build here. He had no idea what he'd do next, whether he really would rebuild or just sell the land as is and move on, perhaps to another town, or maybe a big city where people had never heard his name. Maybe this was fate's way of telling him he'd made a mistake in coming here and that it was time to go.

As soon as that thought occurred to him, he rejected it. In the long run, he might leave Mystic Lake. But not yet, not until he discovered who had risked the lives of everyone living in this town by setting the fire. A few days ago, he'd have had no idea who that person might be. But when Grace had asked him about hate mail he'd received in prison, a name had popped into his head. He'd rejected it at first, but the more he'd thought about it the more it made sense. He'd called his lawyer the other night to ask him to hire an investigator to look into that possibility. If it panned out, Aidan didn't know what he was going to do about it. He just prayed to God that his suspicions were wrong.

He shoved his hand in his jeans pocket for his truck keys, then frowned. He didn't have them. But he'd driven up here by himself…no, with Grace. Did she take the keys and forget to give them to him before she left with the police?

He headed for the truck to see if maybe she'd left the keys in the ignition. But when he opened the driver's door, he stopped in surprise. In the passenger seat, Grace was curled up like a cat, asleep. And in her arms, snugged up against her chest, was the one picture of his family that he'd managed to save from the fire. He didn't even remember her taking it from him. And yet here she was, keeping it safe.

His throat tightened and he crossed to the passenger side of his truck. Careful to open the door as quietly as he could, he eased the picture out of her grasp and slid it under the seat. As he clicked her seat belt in place, she grumbled in her sleep and swatted at his hand, making him smile. Good grief, this woman had a hold on his heart. He didn't want to care about her. It made no sense in such an incredibly short amount of time. But he did care. Not that it mattered.

There wasn't any way that he could be with her without ruining her life as she knew it.

Even if she was willing to give up her career, she shouldn't have to. And being with him would set her up for ridicule and strangers judging her and slighting her. She didn't deserve that. She deserved so much better.

She grumbled in her sleep again, hugging her arms against her chest. With the fire out, the chilly mountain air was moving in. Grace had likely retreated to the truck to keep warm, and here he was standing with the door open making her cold. He eased it shut until it clicked, then crossed to the driver's side. After one last look at what used to be his home, he started his truck and began the slow descent down the mountain.

It turned out that Grace was an incredibly deep sleeper. In spite of all the bumps and turns, she didn't wake up during the drive back to town. She didn't even awaken when Aidan parked his truck behind the B and B. If he didn't have to worry about her reputation and how people would judge her, he'd scoop her up into his arms and carry her to her room. But people *would* judge her. So he leaned into the passenger side of the truck and gently shook her.

She swatted at him again and said a few salty phrases, making him laugh. She might look like an angel, but there was a bit of a devil in her, too. In other words, she was pretty darn perfect.

"Grace," he whispered, not wanting to startle her. "Wake up, Grace. Come on. You can't sleep all night in the truck." He shook her again, harder this time, and her eyes finally fluttered open.

As soon as she saw him, she blinked, then looked around

in confusion. "Aidan? What...where..." Her eyes widened. "We're at the B and B? I don't—"

"The fire was out. You were already in the truck so I buckled your seat belt and drove you home, or, well, to the B and B. Come on. Let's get inside. We both need a shower and some sleep. The sun will be up in a handful of hours. I'm sure it's going to be a long day for both of us."

She nodded, still not seemingly firing on all cylinders. But as she got down from his truck, she suddenly grabbed his arm. "Wait. The picture, it's—"

"Right here." He pulled it out from beneath the seat. "Thanks to you it's safe and sound. I guess I was kind of out of it up on the mountain. You must have realized I was going to drop the frame and you took it to make sure it didn't get broken. Thank you for that. It means a lot. That's the only picture of Elly and Niall that I have. Most of the others burned up in the first fire, twelve years ago. And now, well, that's it unless I can find something in the ruins when I head up later today." He locked the truck. "Do you think you can walk inside on your own?"

She blinked again and shook herself. "Yes, yes. I'm fine. Sorry. Once I get in a deep sleep it's hard for me to wake up. My mom is the same way. I have to put my alarm clock on the other side of my room or I'll turn it off in my sleep. Once I'm on my feet, I'm okay."

"If you say so." He grinned as he followed her inside. She was wobbling like a drunk.

Luckily, there was no one around to see her as they went inside or rumors might have started about her being out late drinking with the town ex-con. But the danger was still very real to her reputation. The reporter was likely in her room. The two of them had to be very quiet as they headed upstairs.

Once Grace's door was open and she stepped inside, he nodded good-night. He was about to turn away when she pressed a hand to his chest, stopping him.

She glanced toward the reporter's room, then leaned in toward him. "Aidan, I'm so sorry for your loss tonight," she whispered. "I know a house can be rebuilt. But the personal items you had can't be replaced. I promise that I'll do everything I can to find out who did this and bring them to justice." She motioned toward the frame he was holding down at his side. "Remember that it's the pictures in your mind, the feelings in your heart, that no one can destroy. The love you have for your family can never be taken away, no matter what anyone says or does."

She started to close the door, but this time he was the one who stopped her.

"Grace," he whispered, his throat tight with emotion. "Thank you for tonight. You were there for me at my darkest, with no concern for what it might cost you. I don't ever want to be the cause of anything bad happening to you. But it means more than you'll ever realize that you were there for me." Unable to resist the impulse, he leaned down and pressed a soft kiss against her lips.

When he pulled back, the melting look she gave him had his body instantly hardening. It was all he could do to leave before he did something they'd both regret.

Chapter Sixteen

While Chief Dawson, Ortiz and Collier spent the morning at the top of the mountain with Aidan searching for anything salvageable from the fire—or evidence pointing to who may have set it—Fletcher stayed at the police station with Grace. They'd spread all of the reports, interviews and pictures from the physical files out on the conference room table as they brainstormed what they had, and didn't have, to prove who was responsible for the bad things happening in Mystic Lake. They also used their laptops to perform searches on law enforcement websites, trying to identify any similar types of recent crimes.

Fletcher sighed and sat back, shaking her head. "I literally have no leads. I mean, we have fingerprints but no match to any known person. Have you gotten any DNA results back from the FBI lab yet?"

"Not yet, but when I spoke to my boss earlier he said he'd call the lab and push them. They should have had enough time to process any DNA profiles by now. I have a feeling they moved other high-priority evidence ahead of mine."

"How can anything possibly be more important than getting DNA to match against your known Crossbow cases?

That will tell you right there whether this killer is operating in our town."

Grace smiled. "That's pretty much what I told my boss. That's why he's calling to put the fear of the *special agent in charge* into the lab. I really do think we'll get something soon."

"I sure hope so. I'd like to know for myself whether we've got a deadly serial killer around here or just some dumb teenager doing stupid stuff. The first one is scary. The second one just makes me mad."

"What exactly do you have against teenagers? You seem to want to blame them for everything that happens around here."

Fletcher snorted. "That's because they generally are. I'm half convinced that most of the spooky, unexplainable things that happen in our town are the result of an evil group of teens on the loose."

"Remind me someday to sit down with you and discuss this prejudice you have against the town's youth and what exactly caused it. But for now, we need to get back to figuring out the case. My boss has granted me another twenty-four hours to try to wrap this up. After that, he's yanking me back to the Knoxville field office to work on something else."

"Ouch. Why is he being such a hard—um, so difficult?"

"I honestly can't fault him. We have a lot of agencies wanting our help on their cases and this one, if it's not related to the killer we're after, will easily be trumped by another more urgent case where people have actually been killed. If the DNA comes back and says your guy isn't my guy, there's no justification for us continuing to spend resources down here."

"Except that we need you."

Grace gave her a doubtful look. "I appreciate that. But you're doing a great job without me. All of the interviews you've conducted and leads you've followed up on are exactly what I'd do. I don't have any secret sauce to solve this thing or I promise I'd share." She pulled the stack of interview reports toward her that she'd been reviewing. "I've noted a few people I'd like to speak to again. But overall, our interviews have yielded pretty much the same answers—that no one has seen any strangers in the area. They don't have any ideas as to who might be terrorizing your town. The best lead right now still seems to be in finding out who is focusing their rage on O'Brien. If we can figure that out, we'll have an excellent suspect to match against our fingerprints and DNA."

Fletcher tapped her nails on the tabletop. "We've been focusing all morning on rehashing the interviews. I'm all for going with your O'Brien angle, that someone's after him. Bring me up to speed on that. I mean, if you think I can help as a sounding board. I don't want to waste your time if you'd rather work it by yourself."

Grace glanced at the glass wall behind Fletcher to make sure no one was around before answering. "If you really don't mind, I'm happy to bore you with my half-baked theories and how I'm looking at this. Maybe you can come up with something I haven't. But we need to keep this just between us to some extent. My thoughts on this aren't flattering to some of the police and I don't want that getting out and offending them."

Fletcher's eyes widened. "Sounds serious. Go ahead. I won't share anything you don't want shared. And you have me dying of curiosity now."

"It's not that big a secret or anything. It's just, well, I'm confused about how the Nashville police handled O'Brien's case."

"You're talking about the murder he committed? And confessed to?"

A surge of annoyance shot through Grace, but she tamped it down. If she hadn't met Aidan and considered herself an excellent judge of character, she'd no doubt feel the same way as Fletcher. She'd assume Aidan really was a murderer. But the case didn't make sense to her and she couldn't see him killing his wife. If she'd harbored even a shred of doubt about that, it had evaporated last night when she'd seen him hugging that picture of his wife and son after nearly getting killed in order to save it from the fire.

"I'm referring to his past, and yes, my research into the investigation of Elly O'Brien's death. My goal is to come up with a list of people who hate him enough to try to frame him at the festival, and for shooting an arrow at me."

"Speaking of which, are you doing okay? You don't seem to be favoring your hurt arm."

"Thanks to over-the-counter pain pills, I'm really good. It only hurt a lot the first night. As for my list of potential suspects, I looked into any issues he had in prison. Like if he had altercations with some of the other prisoners, made any enemies who are now out of prison and trying to pay him back for some real or imagined slight."

"I bet that's a long list," Fletcher said. "Ten years in prison for a convicted murderer no doubt means there are a lot of guys he didn't get along with. He's proven to be predisposed to violence. So I'm sure he didn't put up with anything from the other men while in there."

Once again, Grace felt a surge of annoyance at the policewoman. It was becoming harder and harder to hide her anger. But she did, or hoped she did.

"Actually, he was a model prisoner. There were zero fights on his record. He seemed to get along with everyone as best as could be expected."

"Huh. Surprising. So no suspects from prison then? No one's name to add to a list?"

"Not fellow prisoners, no. Although I did have an admin dig into that a little more for me to see which prisoners he may have known at the time who were recently released, or at least released since O'Brien was paroled. There were a few, but they all came up clean. Actually, two of them re-offended almost immediately and are now back in prison, which clears them since they couldn't have been in Mystic Lake during the festival. But the others we researched have checked out so far as it being unlikely they could have been here to cause any trouble. That leaves visitors or people from O'Brien's past from before he went to prison. That list is a lot longer to go through. He owns his own business and knows a lot of people through that, in addition to those he called friends before his wife's death, and his former in-laws of course. I'm still going through that list. I've made some calls, but of course haven't been able to go to Nashville just yet to follow up in person."

"How many people are we talking?" Fletcher asked.

"His company in Nashville on average has about a hundred people on payroll, far more if you consider other locations. But I'm focusing on Nashville first since that's where he used to live and he would have met a lot, if not all of those workers. Most of them are long-term employees who were there back when O'Brien was convicted. Any one of them could hold a grudge for some reason or other. That's in addition to the twenty-plus friends and his in-laws."

She whistled. "That's a huge list. I'd probably focus on the friends and in-laws first."

"Agreed. I've already looked into the friends. Nothing came of it. I'm looking into the in-laws right now."

"So we need to whittle the other hundred or so down. I'd look for workers' comp claims in case they blame him for injuries. Maybe human resource complaints about unfair practices, things like that. I'd look into promotions and who might resent him for choosing someone else over them. Seems petty, but when it comes to people's salaries, that stuff gets pretty personal."

"All of those are great suggestions. I'd also like to see whether anyone has been fired who might blame him."

"If you want, I can work those angles," Fletcher offered. "I worked my only local investigation yesterday to get it out of the way, a petty theft at the grocery store."

"*The* grocery store? There's only one in town?"

Fletcher laughed. "Pretty much there's only one of anything in this town. Guess who the culprit ended up being?"

Grace sat back to think, but the grin on the other woman's face told her the answer. "One of those evil teenagers. Am I right?"

"A hundred percent. I wanted to arrest him and make him cool his jets in our holding cell for a day or two. But the chief made me check with the store manager first. The guy had no backbone. Didn't want to press charges once he heard it was a fifteen-year-old. So I did what I end up having to do most of the time around here. I went to the kid's home and spoke to him with his parents present, putting the fear of the almighty police into him. He swore he'd never do it again. But his parents were so quick to pony up the money to pay for what their kid had done that he likely didn't learn a thing. I'll probably have to scare him again in another month or two."

Fletcher held out her hand. "Give me what you have—the prison visitor logs for O'Brien, the employee lists, all of it. I'm begging you. I'd love to speak to some adults and put the fear in them for a change. It'll be fun."

"Emailing it to you now."

"Awesome. Wait, you said there was something about the Nashville police that had you concerned. Did one of them hold a grudge against O'Brien, maybe beat him up or fabricate evidence? You think a police officer could be our suspect?"

"No, no. Nothing like that. It's more a question about the investigation that was performed after Elly O'Brien's death. The police reports are insufficient, really thin. And they didn't dig very deep. I'm just surprised, and disappointed, in the lack of depth of their research. Normally, they're a top-notch agency. But in this particular case, they didn't dig like I'd expect."

"O'Brien confessed. They didn't need to spend additional resources on the case. Makes sense to me."

Grace nodded, pretending to agree with her. Fletcher's obvious bias against O'Brien—which again she fully understood—made it difficult to expect any neutrality in looking at who might have it in for him. Rather than go into more detail about her concerns, she decided to keep those thoughts to herself.

"It's been bothering me," Grace said. "But I see your point. Are you sure you want to dig into that huge list I sent you?"

"Are you kidding? This is my catnip, something different to dig my teeth into. If one of these guys is our suspect, I'll find out. However, it's going to have to wait until after lunch. I'm meeting a friend at Stella's restaurant." She grinned. "It's a guy friend or I'd invite you to come along."

"No worries. I don't want to be a third wheel. I'll order something from that sandwich shop. Is it okay for me to stay here by myself or do you need to lock up and switch the phone lines like you do at night?"

Fletcher's expression flattened with disappointment. "I didn't even think about that. You're becoming like one of our team. Normally, Collier or Ortiz would cover me for lunch. But I don't know how much longer they'll—"

The outer door opened and two men entered the police station, Collier and Aidan. A rush of pleasure shot through Grace at seeing Aidan, until she noticed the grim look in his eyes. The hunt for any personal items to have survived the fire must not have gone well.

"Looks like your lunch is salvaged," she said. "Collier's back."

Fletcher turned around in her chair, then shot to her feet. "For once, I'm actually happy to see him. Later, Grace." She rushed out of the conference room and after a brief chat with her fellow officer was out the door.

Grace locked her laptop, then left the conference room to greet Collier and Aidan. "How did it go? I'm guessing from your expressions, not very well?"

They both shook their heads. Collier said, "No evidence so far that might point to who set the fire. But it's early yet."

"What about you...O'Brien?" She'd just caught herself in time not to call him Aidan in front of Collier. "Any luck finding anything salvageable?"

"The fire department had to put out some hot spots that were smoking to make sure the fire didn't reignite. Because of that, I couldn't look for anything. I'll go back in a few hours and see if the fire marshal allows me to search then."

"Hopefully he will."

"She," Collier corrected. "Lieutenant Molly Graham. She was the marshal on call and drove in from Chattanooga. I'm thinking maybe I'll ask her to dinner later. You know, as a local courtesy from one agency to another."

Aidan smiled at that, apparently having heard about Collier's reputation as a ladies' man.

"Have you two had lunch?" Grace asked. "I'm about to head to that sandwich shop down the block. You're welcome to join me."

"You go ahead," Collier said. "I'm on duty. Can't leave the station unless another officer is here. Maybe bring O'Brien and me something back if you don't mind, after you finish your lunch. Hot ham and cheese sounds good. Tell them to put it on the station's tab. O'Brien, what do you want her to get for you?"

Aidan looked as disappointed as Grace felt. Perhaps he'd forgotten for a moment, like her, that the two of them going to a café together might not be the best idea.

"Ham and cheese works for me, too. Thanks, Special Agent Malone."

She nodded and hurried to the café. Eating there wasn't something she planned to do if Aidan wasn't with her. Instead, she grabbed their lunch to go and headed back to the station.

"Here you go, Collier. O'Brien, I'd like to reinterview you, ask some more questions to try to figure out who has it out for you. If you don't mind a working lunch, you and I can sit in the conference room. Sound good?"

"Sure. Happy to help."

Collier looked like he was about to offer to join them, but Grace led the way to the conference room and shut the door behind her and Aidan. When Collier didn't follow them inside, she figured he must have gotten the hint.

Chapter Seventeen

They both took a few minutes to spread out their lunch on the table, her facing the glass wall so she could keep an eye on Collier and any eavesdropping or lipreading he might want to do, and Aidan sitting across from her.

Once Collier was diving into his food and surfing the web as an apparent lunchtime diversion, Grace quickly swallowed down the bite she'd just taken and took a sip from her water bottle before setting it aside.

"How are you holding up, Aidan?" She kept her voice low so it wouldn't carry through the glass.

He smiled. "I figured this wasn't about a reinterview. Don't worry about me. I've been through far worse."

"Well, of course I worry about you. You've been through so much hardship. It's not right that some nut has his sights set on making life even more difficult for you. My boss is threatening to pull me off this case if I can't prove a link to the Crossbow Killer soon. But that's not going to stop me from working on this investigation. I'll do it on my own time. I'm going to prove you had nothing to do with this, or anything else."

He stared at her in silence, his brows drawn down in a

frown. Then he slowly shook his head, his expression a mix between confusion and something else. Anger? Fear? What?

"Malone—"

"You've had your tongue down my throat and vice versa. You can call me Grace."

He laughed, but quickly sobered. "Fair enough. I can understand why I'm attracted to you. You're smart, funny and beautiful for starters. But I can't even begin to understand why a special agent with the FBI would not only be attracted to me, but also seems to trust me. Why are you so determined to look into my case? Why do you insist on trying to prove that I didn't commit a crime to which I confessed and spent ten years in prison? I didn't appeal or try to have my sentence reduced. If I'm not trying to prove I'm innocent, why are you?"

"Well, first, thanks for saying I'm smart, funny and beautiful. You left out sexy, by the way, but I'll forgive you."

He choked on another laugh and shook his head.

"Second, the reason I'm so convinced you're innocent of any crime is precisely because I'm an FBI agent and a former cop. I'm experienced in reading people and facts. Your actions speak to your character. You've done nothing but help people from the moment we met, even the police who haven't exactly been nice to you since you came here. But it's what I've found and haven't found when looking into your past as part of trying to figure out who is trying to frame you for the crimes here in Mystic Lake that raise so many questions as to make it seem ludicrous that you could have killed your wife."

After another long silence, he crossed his arms. "All right. I'll bite. What makes it seem impossible to you that I'm actually guilty of murder?"

Excited that he was finally at least willing to listen to her about his case, and hopeful that she could get him to discuss it, she thumbed through a stack of manila folders and then pulled out the thinnest one from the middle. She slid it across the table toward him.

He picked it up, but hesitated without opening it. "What is this?"

"A printout of Nashville PD's complete investigation into the death of Elly O'Brien."

He dropped the folder onto the table as if it had burned his hand. "I don't need to read that. I know what happened."

"Care to share that knowledge with me?"

"Didn't we already have this conversation at my cabin, the day you were at my workshop admiring the table I was building? I told you about what happened the day...the day Elly passed."

"You told me what you told the police years ago. But I'm not convinced that's the truth, or at least not the whole truth." She picked up the folder and flipped it open. "There are a total of twenty-five pages in here. And that includes the eight-page autopsy report."

He winced, then cleared his throat. "Your point?"

"The police didn't even try to corroborate your so-called confession. I've never, not once, seen a file this incomplete for an investigation of any kind, let alone an alleged murder. Which led me to wonder whether you were threatened by the police and framed—"

"No to both."

"Okay. I'll accept that answer for now. Then the question becomes why would the police be so quick to take your confession and not look deeper, and of course the other glaring question of why would you confess to something you didn't do?"

"Grace—"

"The answer to the first is obvious once you look really closely at the file. There's an obscure handwritten note that I didn't notice right away because it's on a printout of a copy to begin with. It's not very clear and part of it was chopped off in the margin." She flipped through the file and pulled out a single page and pointed to the right edge. "See that?"

He eyed the page as if it were a snake. "Not really, but I'm sure you're going to tell me."

Sighing, she pointed to some grainy handwriting. "I actually had to borrow a magnifying glass from Fletcher to read it myself. It says, 'Parents of deceased request speedy end to case so family can move on and heal. Prosecutor agrees.'"

He shrugged.

"Come on, Aidan. You know where I'm going with this. The odds of a DA agreeing to halt an investigation without corroborating your confession are about zero. They must have had pressure from both the parents *and the defense*. Your attorney had to have been consulted about this. If not, he could have argued to the court that the investigation was rushed and insufficient and requested that your case be dismissed. Heck, he could have easily argued that if you really did unplug your wife's ventilator that you weren't in your right mind, that you did it to show her mercy. Without a criminal record and this being your first offense, he could have brought forth witnesses to talk about your relationship with Elly and how madly in love you were. But he didn't, even though everyone I've called and spoken to says exactly that, how close you were. Your attorney could have said you were in despair seeing her in pain, paralyzed, unable to breathe on her own, and that it clouded your judgment. Even I could have probably gotten you a reduced sentence and I'm not an attorney. Yours didn't call one single witness at your sentencing, which happened just a few days after that report was written up with that note in the margin."

She waited, but when he didn't say anything, she continued. "As you pointed out earlier, you never submitted any appeals even though you had a strong case for one based on insufficient evidence. That all leads me to believe that you probably colluded with your wife's parents to bring the case to an end prematurely."

He crossed his arms on top of the table. "So what if I did? Dragging it out would only hurt them even more. Bringing the case to a quick close was the least I could do."

"And nothing a little bribery from a wealthy man couldn't handle, is that it?"

His jaw tightened.

"Right. No comment. Let's skip to the second part of my earlier question, the part about why you would confess to a crime you didn't do. That one has had me stumped, but I'm working it out. For one thing, I tried to get a transcript from your parole hearing to find out what was said and who spoke at the hearing."

His eyes widened and for the first time since coming into the conference room, he looked worried.

"In spite of repeated attempts by both me and an admin, we haven't gotten the transcripts. They've been sealed. That's pretty dang convenient for you if you're trying to hide the truth that may have come out during the hearing."

His brow smoothed out and he seemed to visibly relax

after she'd said she couldn't get the transcript. Time to go for the jugular.

"The admin did, however, manage to get the prison's visitor log for the date of your appearance before the parole board."

His eyes widened.

"It's not a surprise that your wife's parents were at the hearing, until you consider one thing. Typically, if the family of a convicted murderer is at the first parole hearing and argues against parole, the board goes along with their wishes. But they didn't come to speak against you, did they? They spoke on your behalf—whether you wanted them to or not. That's why you were paroled. Which tells me that Elly's parents don't believe you killed their daughter any more than I do. Something changed their mind during the ten years that you were in prison. They found out the truth about what really happened, didn't they?"

His face paled. "Grace. Don't."

She swore. "I knew it. Your reaction just confirmed it. What's more, you lied to me about her parents when you said they hated you. They may have, at first, but definitely not toward the end of your incarceration. That's based not only on you being paroled and my conclusions around that, but hard facts I dug up about them. I didn't find one single thing that makes me believe they're the type of people who'd try to frame you as the Crossbow Killer, or even hire someone else to do it. So where does that leave us?"

"Grace—"

"Fact. Elly's parents used to think you were the killer. Fact. They now are certain you're innocent. If that wasn't true, they wouldn't have testified for your early release before the parole board. Fact. Everything I've read about them confirms they loved and doted on their daughter, so there's no question they'd want her killer to face justice. But they haven't gone to the police to request that the investigation be reopened to find her real killer. Why not?"

He let out a shuddering breath but remained silent.

"The only logical conclusion in light of all those facts is that Elly's parents know the identity of her killer and don't want him punished." She held up her hands. "Why in the world wouldn't they want him brought to justice? Why wouldn't you?"

He squeezed his eyes shut as if in pain.

She reached across the table and put her hand on his arm, no longer caring whether Collier noticed. When Aidan's eyes flew open, the anguish in them was almost enough to make her stop. Almost. But she couldn't, not when she was so close to finding out the truth.

"Aidan. Who are you and your dead wife's parents covering for? And why?"

He stared at her hand on his arm, his throat working. Finally, he looked up, his eyes clouded with despair. "I'm begging you. Let it go. The truth won't make anyone feel any better. It will only cause more pain. Please. Stop."

Her throat tightened with the urge to weep. But she held fast. "The last thing I want to do is hurt you. But this isn't just about you, or even justice for your wife at this point. Someone is trying to destroy you. And I'm betting it's the same person you're trying to protect. It's the only thing that makes sense when you look at everything that's happened."

"You don't know that," he whispered, his voice ragged and raw. "There's no proof."

"Do you expect me to believe that you've been protecting a killer all these years, and now that you're out of prison he's not the same killer who's trying to send you back? You see what he's doing, right? He's worried you're going to try to clear your name by finally telling the police what you've known all along. He tried to frame you first by almost killing two men in a boat. Then he shot at me, twice. When he burned down your house last night, do you think he went inside first to make sure you weren't there? Hell, no. He hoped you were there and would be trapped and killed. Why would you want to protect someone like that?"

She searched his gaze, then delivered her last volley. "He already killed your wife. Who does he have to kill for you to finally do something about him?"

He made a strangled sound in his throat and pulled his hand free. "You think you have it figured out, Grace. But you don't. He didn't… He was too… Elly's death isn't his fault."

She stared at him in shock, his words bouncing around inside her brain like a Ping-Pong ball as things started to mesh together in her mind. She'd made one of the worst mistakes a law enforcement officer could make. Tunnel vision. She'd come up with a theory and had used the evidence to support her theory. Instead, she should have examined the evidence and let it reveal a theory.

Aidan stared at her, his handsome face drawn in lines of worry, frustration and a soul-deep sadness as he waited for the inevitability of her fitting all of the pieces together. She laid the evidence out in her mind's eye. In the end, it was so simple, so obvious, she was embarrassed that she hadn't realized it on day one of looking into Aidan's past. It was the fact that he'd confessed that had thrown her off. But even that should have been a glaring clue to the truth. So. Ridiculously. Obvious.

Aidan didn't kill Elly.

There was no evidence of an intruder.

Elly was paralyzed and couldn't have done anything.

Someone else pulled the plug on her ventilator.

The nurse had gone home for the day, leaving Elly's care to Aidan.

But Aidan wasn't the only person in the house after she left.

Aidan's words, just moments ago, flitted through her mind.

"He didn't... He was too... Elly's death isn't his fault."

She filled in the missing words that he hadn't said.

He didn't *understand what he was doing.* He was too *young.* Elly's death isn't his fault.

She stared at him, the last of it becoming clear. "The hate mail," she whispered. "Elly's parents found out about it, read the letters. And then they knew the truth. That's why they wanted to help you, but didn't want the police to reinvestigate."

He squeezed his hands into fists on top of the table and bowed his head.

"Niall," she said. "Your son. He pulled the plug. He killed Elly and now he wants to kill you to keep the truth from coming out."

He jerked his head up, frowning. "He was five years old, Grace. He doesn't even remember doing it. He remembers bits and pieces, just enough from that day to have made Elly's parents suspicious that something was off because what he said didn't match what I said. That's why they visited me years later, trying to understand what really happened."

"And that's why they supported your parole."

He nodded.

"Why not just tell the truth from the beginning? No one's going to prosecute a five-year-old child for pulling a cord out of a wall. He didn't realize what he was doing."

"It's more complicated than that."

"Then explain it to me. If your son isn't here to keep you from telling the truth, then he must be here for payback, revenge for killing his mom, right? After you were paroled, he must have gone on a hunt or maybe even hired a private investigator to find out where you were. Then he came after you. If that's the case, then why protect him?"

"Because he's my son." His voice broke, and he cleared his throat.

She stared at him as the truth came out, more shaken than she cared to admit. After a few calming breaths, she continued, determined to get the whole story, finally.

"Okay. I get that. I really do. I get that you want to protect him now, here as the copycat, to keep him from going to prison. I don't agree with it. But I understand it. What still confuses me is why you confessed to your wife's murder when it would have been so simple to tell the truth that your five-year-old son accidentally pulled the plug on her machine."

"Like I said," his voice was raw, strained. "It's more complicated than that. For one thing, I didn't want Niall to grow up knowing he'd helped to kill his own mother. It could have destroyed his life."

"Wait. Helped? I don't... Are you saying that you—"

"No." He shook his head. "No, Grace. You've been right all along about that. I never would have done anything to hurt Elly. I didn't go to prison just to protect my son. I went to prison because—"

The door to the conference room burst open, startling

both of them. Fletcher entered the room, holding a piece of paper.

Grace swore. "Fletcher, we're in the middle of something here—"

"I know. Collier told me. My lunch date canceled and I came back to work on that list we talked about. You didn't even notice I was in the squad room because of whatever you two are talking so intently about in here." She gave Aidan the kind of look that someone would give a bug crawling across the floor right before they squashed it. Or a police officer would give to a man they believed had committed murder.

Fletcher pitched the piece of paper onto the table in front of him. "That's a summary of visitor log entries from your time in prison, all ten years. Malone reviewed them, trying to figure out who has it out for you. But she didn't realize something that you and I know—that one of the people on that list visited you several times in the early years of your incarceration, and again the day of your parole hearing. Malone didn't realize the significance because she didn't recognize the name, probably hadn't had time to research it yet. But you and I know that your visitor got married after moving to Mystic Lake. So tell me, why did Stella Simmons, married name Stella Holman, visit you in prison?"

His eyes narrowed at her, his jaw tight.

Grace flattened her palms on top of the table. "Wait, Stella and Aidan were friends before he went to prison?"

Fletcher's brows shot up. "Since when did you start calling him by his first name?"

Grace's face heated. "You've heard of building rapport with someone you're interviewing, right?"

Fletcher's eye roll told Grace she didn't buy that excuse. "Whatever. I don't have all the answers yet, but something stinks to high heaven here. Stella and O'Brien have never mentioned to anyone in Mystic Lake that I'm aware of that they used to know each other, long before he moved here. So I put two and two together. Stella was a nurse, in Nashville, before she came to this town. Guess what type of nurse? The kind who works in people's homes to help them care for homebound patients."

Grace stared at Aidan. "Like Elly?"

He gave her a sharp look. "She was one of Elly's nurses. What's that got to do with anything?"

Fletcher snorted. "Your wife died because something happened to her life support machine, or whatever. Stella was one of her nurses. Then you just happen to move to Mystic Lake after you get out of prison, the same place where Stella moved. If I was a betting woman, I'd bet a year's salary you two are covering up something."

"And what would that be?" he demanded, his tone sarcastic. "I already went to prison for murder. There's nothing worse than that."

"Aidan?" Grace was barely able to force the next words out. "Is Stella the one who pulled the plug on the ventilator? Is that the complicated part you spoke about?"

His eyes darkened with anger. "No."

Fletcher held up her hands. "Whoa, whoa. Wait a minute. I thought we were trying to figure out who has a grudge against O'Brien. What are you doing, Malone? Trying to exonerate him or something?"

Aidan stood, towering over Fletcher. She immediately took several steps back, her hand going to her holster.

He gave her a disgusted look. "We're done here." He brushed past her and yanked open the door.

Grace jumped to her feet. "Aidan, wait. Please."

But he was already gone.

Chapter Eighteen

Aidan paced back and forth in his room at the B and B. He'd worked so hard to hide the truth, had spent ten long, horrific years in prison to do so. And now everything was unraveling. He wanted to hate Grace for pulling at the threads, for refusing to stop in spite of him practically begging her to do so. But he could never hate her. As impossible as it seemed, he was half in love with her. She was the only person besides Stella who'd believed in his innocence almost from the very start. Grace believed him to be a decent man. And that felt too good to ignore.

Even though she was destroying everything he'd worked so hard to build.

He'd already spoken to Stella, to warn her that Grace knew the truth, or at least part of it. Now the question was what to do next. How could he protect the people he cared about without endangering anyone else? Was the person here in Mystic Lake the one he'd been protecting all along? Or was it this Crossbow Killer Grace had come here to find? And, oh God please no, were the two of them one and the same?

He slumped down onto the bed, his head in his hands. All these years he'd thought his decision that first day was the best way to salvage a disastrous situation. But what if it wasn't? Stella had certainly never agreed with the path he'd taken. She'd tried so hard to talk him out of it. Had she been right all along? Had his cover-up only made things worse? Would everything have turned out for the better if he'd faced the truth from the start? Embraced it and figured out another way to move forward? To atone for his own sins, as well?

Second-guessing the past wasn't doing anyone any good. He had to focus on now, to figure out how to stop whoever was stalking Mystic Lake, and him, whether it was his son or someone else. Grace had already been hurt. And others could have been hurt, or killed, when his home was burned. It was only a matter of time before someone was going to get killed.

Unless he did something to end this.

The lies were unraveling. The truth was coming out. It was time to accept that he couldn't cover it up anymore. Time to fix what he'd broken all those years ago. Somehow. Without making it even worse.

But to fix it, first, he needed to know if Grace was right. He had to know whether his perfect little boy, his son, had become the monster that Grace believed him to be.

He pulled his cell phone out of his pocket and speed-dialed his lawyer. "Hi, Nate. Yeah, it's me. Have you had a chance to look into what we spoke about?" He listened as his lawyer put the last nail in the coffin.

Niall had left the Larsens' Henderson, Kentucky, home a week ago.

His credit card purchases showed he'd driven to Tennessee and had spent several days in a Chattanooga hotel. He'd made purchases at a camping supply store, and bought a crossbow and several quivers of arrows. Another purchase was made at a party store, where he'd bought a large bag of white feathers and red craft paint. The last damning fact the lawyer shared was that Niall checked out of the hotel the morning of the festival. There had been no other charges on his card since then.

He was in Mystic Lake. Had to be. He was the one with his sights set on Aidan, with innocent people's lives at stake for just being in the same location.

"Nate." Aidan cleared his tight throat. "Could he be... do you think he's this Crossbow Killer they've been talking about on the news?"

His longtime lawyer, who'd also become a good friend over the years, told him what he'd feared and prayed wasn't true.

"Could he be? Logistically, it's possible, Aidan. It's a five-hour drive from his grandparents' home in Henderson to Knoxville where the murders have taken place. I looked into the dates of each of the six killings so far—"

"Six. My God."

"We don't know it's your son, Aidan. Have some hope."

"I've been trying, believe me. Go on. You looked into the killings and what?"

"All of them have happened on a weekend."

"Which works with Aidan's schedule since there wouldn't be any school absences to explain. Maybe the Larsens can prove he has an alibi for at least some of those dates. A family trip or something like that."

"Is that what you want, Aidan? You want me to contact them?"

Aidan thought about it, then straightened, his heart heavy. "I don't see how we can avoid it anymore. Niall's in a world of trouble for what he's done here in Mystic Lake. He'll need the only parents he's ever really known to help him through this. He'll need a lawyer."

"I can help his parents get one."

"I'm speaking to one of the best defense attorneys in the country."

Nate sighed. "I only wish you'd allowed me to be the best back when all this started, with you."

"You did what your client wanted. No one can hold that against you. Will you help Niall? If the Larsens agree?"

"Of course. I'd love a chance to keep an O'Brien out of prison instead of helping him into one. It would be my honor."

"Thanks."

"What are you going to do now, Aidan? What's your next step?"

His hand tightened around the phone. "I'm going to find my son."

GRACE SAT ALONE in the conference room. Fletcher had made no secret that she wasn't happy with her "friendliness" toward Aidan, as the policewoman had called it. Once Aidan had left, Fletcher had given Grace a look of censure, then returned to her desk. But, thankfully, she was still helping with the case. Fletcher had called Grace half a dozen times in the past twenty minutes to ask about entries on the list she was researching. That left Grace free to explore other leads.

Like finally viewing the lab results.

She'd just received an email that they were ready, so she excitedly pulled them up on her laptop.

The reports were detailed and full of geek-speak, so it

took a while to cull through them. She made notes as she went, and then checked her list.

Shoe prints from the festival matched shoe prints taken up on the mountain at Aidan's place. Fingerprints on each of the arrows retrieved from the boat, the woods and the one that had struck Grace's arm all matched one another. That was enough evidence to prove that the same person had struck both the festival and the mountain at Aidan's place. Although it really wasn't a surprise, it was a relief to have something solid, actual facts instead of conjecture. But what she really wanted to know was whether the Mystic Lake suspect was the Crossbow Killer.

She scrolled through page after page of measurements of arrows and feathers and paint chemicals as well as comparisons of types of shoes and sizes that could have left the print. Finally, she came to the part she most wanted to see.

The DNA results.

The FBI had already added the DNA profile of the Crossbow Killer into CODIS. The lab had submitted the profile from the Mystic Lake shooter to CODIS to search for a match.

They got one.

Grace read the lab report again, then reread it slowly to make sure she was interpreting everything correctly.

She was.

She locked her laptop, grabbed her jacket and rushed from the conference room.

Fletcher, who was on the phone, called for her to wait as she ran for the door. But Grace didn't stop. She had to talk to Aidan.

Chapter Nineteen

The sound of a snapping twig had Aidan whirling around. He slowly straightened as Grace emerged from between two trees.

"What the— Grace, what are you doing here?" He scanned the woods surrounding them.

"They're not with me," she assured him. "I spoke to Dawson and Ortiz when I got here. They had just rendez-voused at the ruins of your cabin to confer about where to search next for our bow and arrow guy. They told me this section was where you were looking."

He scanned the woods again. "I'm not worried about where the police are. I'm worried about where the shooter might be. Please tell me you're wearing your Kevlar vest under your jacket."

She glanced down and grimaced. "Actually, no. I was hot earlier and hung it on my chair at the station. Didn't even think about it when I went looking for you."

He swore beneath his breath. "Then put mine on."

She stopped him from shrugging out of his coat to remove his vest by pressing her hand against his chest. "No. No way will I take your vest. If something happened to you, I couldn't live with that guilt."

"Then you're leaving. Now. Let's go." He grabbed her arm.

She pulled away from him and frowned. "I'll leave you to your searching in a minute. But I need to tell you something first."

What she didn't realize was that he was doing everything he could to make himself a target to lure the shooter out into the open. He was still clinging to a tiny shred of doubt that Niall was the shooter. But if he was, then Aidan had to do everything he could to make sure he was brought in safe and sound. He couldn't leave the capture of his son to the police who might be trigger-happy when confronted with a man with a deadly crossbow. The problem was, if Aiden standing on exposed cliffs and loudly stomping around the creeks and streams on his property in the areas where it made sense that someone might camp out or hide had attracted any attention, then his son was on his way right now to confront him.

And Grace could get caught in the cross fire.

"Talk to me while I escort you back to your vehicle," Aidan said, reaching for her again.

She jerked her arm away and frowned at him. "All right, all right. But stop grabbing me like you're about to throw me over your knee and spank me."

He coughed to hide a smile. "You don't like to be spanked. Good to know."

She rolled her eyes.

He scanned the path and trees again, then motioned for her to walk beside him.

"I got the results back from the FBI lab," she told him.

His stomach dropped. "Go on." His throat was tight as he waited to find out whether his theory about the shooter's identity was right.

"They confirm the man we're after is the one from the festival, and everything happening up here at your place."

"You knew that already."

"I suspected it. Now there's proof in the form of shoe-print analysis, fingerprint analysis and DNA."

He stopped. "DNA?"

"A full profile. The lab entered it into CODIS—that's the—"

"FBI DNA database. I know. When I confessed to Elly's murder they took my DNA sample and added my profile to that same database." He started forward again, his hand on the small of her back urging her to keep moving.

"The FBI has entered the Crossbow Killer's DNA into CODIS, too, from the crime scenes already attributed to him. The hope is that a suspect will eventually be identified to match against that profile at some point. But when the lab submitted the Mystic Lake shooter's profile it didn't come back as a match to the Crossbow Killer."

"Did *not* come back as a match?"

"Not even close. The anonymous call about the Crossbow Killer being in Mystic Lake was wrong. The suspect for these local events is someone else entirely. Which supports my theory that the Mystic Lake shooting suspect is probably the same person who submitted that anonymous tip in the first place, because he was trying to frame you and send you back to prison."

He held up a low-hanging branch to let her through, then joined her again on the path. "You came all the way up here and hiked a quarter mile through the woods to tell me the suspect all of us are chasing isn't the Crossbow Killer? That information could have waited."

"True. But *this* couldn't. I wanted to make sure you knew before you heard it from someone else. The DNA profile—"

"Malone? You out here?" Fletcher's voice rang through the woods somewhere ahead.

"Good grief. She's determined I shouldn't be around you," Grace said. "I'm here," she called out. "We're coming toward you."

"Okay," Fletcher called back.

"The DNA profile?" Aidan asked, stepping over a fallen log then lifting Grace over it.

She smiled her thanks, but put her hand on his chest, stopping him.

"Grace, we need to get going."

"Just one minute, okay?" She kept her voice low. "I want to tell you this before we reach Fletcher."

He sighed and looked around, actively watching the woods. "Hurry. Tell me what's so important."

"Our suspect's DNA wasn't a match to the Crossbow Killer. But it was a partial match, a familial match to another profile in the database. There were thirteen core DNA loci between the two, which is why CODIS spit it out."

He felt the blood drain from his face. "Familial?"

She looked at him with such sympathy that it nearly broke him.

"Just say it, Grace."

"The partial match was to you. The suspect, the one here in Mystic Lake, is related to you by blood. He shares 50 percent of your DNA. I'm so sorry. It's no longer just a theory. The shooter we're looking for is definitely Niall. Your son."

"I knew it," he whispered, barely able to get out the words. "But hearing it from you, knowing there's no room for doubt anymore, makes it so much worse."

She reached her hands up and cupped his face, her gaze searching his. "I'm so sorry, Aidan."

He gently tugged her arms down, even though he wanted nothing more right now than to find solace in the arms of this amazing woman. But he couldn't allow his selfish needs or desires put her at risk for another second. "We really have to go. I've done everything I can to draw out the—to draw out my son if he's hiding on my property. You can't be out here without your vest to at least offer some partial protection."

Her eyes widened. "What did you do to draw him out?"

He grabbed her hand and tugged her forward. "Everything but shout a dare from the top of the mountain. Maybe I'll do that next, after you're somewhere safe."

"Oh, Aidan. I wish you wouldn't be so careless about your own safety. You shouldn't—"

"Malone? Where are you?" Fletcher walked around some bushes and stopped when she saw Aidan. Her gaze flitted down to where Aidan was holding Grace's hand.

Aidan tugged his hand free, ignoring Grace's unhappy frown. He motioned toward Fletcher. "You brought Malone's vest?"

Grace blinked as if just now realizing that Fletcher was holding it.

"Of course," Fletcher said. "She ran out of the station without it, risking her life to come find you, I might add. I called Dawson and he told me where you were, so I figured that's where she'd go." She gave Grace a hard look. "Even though you aren't answering your phone."

"Sorry," Grace said. "When I saw you calling I turned off the ringer. I had something else on my mind and didn't want to lose my focus."

Fletcher snorted. "It's obvious what, or who, you had on your mind. You didn't want to hear me say anything bad about him. That's why you didn't answer."

Aidan stepped forward and took the vest from her. "Thank you for bringing this." He turned to Grace. "Over or under your jacket?"

She blew out a frustrated breath. "Under. Give me a second." She quickly worked at her buttons.

The barest whisper of sound had Aidan whirling toward the woods off to his left, searching for the source. A flash of white through the trees was his only warning. "Get down," he yelled, diving toward Fletcher and throwing her to the ground.

"He's here," Grace yelled into her phone as she scrambled behind a tree and yanked out her gun. "Dawson, the suspect just shot at Fletcher."

The policewoman was lying on the ground, looking stunned as she stared up at the arrow embedded in a thick oak tree just past where she'd been standing moments ago. "My God," she said. "That would have gone right through my head if you hadn't knocked me down."

Aidan grabbed her shoulders and yanked her behind the cover of a thick tree. "You'll have another chance to die if you don't pay attention and use your training. He's still out there."

Fletcher stared at him, then blew out a shaky breath. "Okay, okay. Right. Which way did he—"

A young man stepped out from behind a thick bush not far from Grace. The same young man Aidan only got to see in a new picture once a year through his lawyer.

Niall.

He was aiming his crossbow at Aidan.

Niall sneered. "Finally, after all these years." A single tear coursed down his cheek. "Killed anyone else's mom lately?"

"Drop it!" Grace yelled, aiming her gun at Niall.

"No," Aidan shouted. "Don't."

Niall whirled toward her, still holding his bow.

"Son, don't do it." Aidan jumped to his feet.

Bam!

A red wet spot appeared on Niall's shirt and quickly began to spread across his chest. His eyes widened in surprise as he fell to the ground, his bow landing harmlessly beside him.

Aidan froze, then looked at Grace in horror.

"No," she whispered. "I didn't shoot."

He turned and saw Fletcher still sitting on the ground, her pistol in her hands, pointed at his son.

"Dad?" A pitiful, confused rasp broke through Aidan's shock. "Daddy?"

"I'm here, son. Daddy's here." He dropped to his knees and desperately pressed his hands against Niall's wound to try to stop the bleeding. As if through a long, deep tunnel, he registered the sounds of Grace calling 911 for an ambulance and Fletcher calling Dawson, telling him they needed help. But all of that faded at the horror of feeling his son's lifeblood seeping through his fingers.

Chapter Twenty

As Aidan sat beside Niall's hospital bed, watching his chest rise and fall, he couldn't help but wonder at the miracle that his anonymous donation to buy Mystic Lake a medevac chopper had saved his son's life. Two days after the shooting, Niall was still miraculously clinging to life in the intensive care unit at a Chattanooga hospital.

He was in a medically induced coma to help his body heal. But he was breathing on his own now. Seeing him on a ventilator that first day had nearly destroyed Aidan. He didn't think he could survive watching another loved one suffer the way Elly had. But Niall was young. And he was a fighter.

He'd need that fighting spirit not only to bounce back physically, but to live down the toxic lies the media was spreading. The reporter who'd been staying at the B and B had announced that the Crossbow Killer had been operating in Mystic Lake and that he was now clinging to life at the hospital after being shot by police. Aidan was grateful that his son's name had been suppressed in the news reports because he was a minor. But in today's world of social media, someone would leak his name eventually and it would spread across cyberspace.

A tap on the large glass window to the hallway had him looking up to see Grace, looking nervous and somber beside her boss, Dawson, Aidan's lawyer and friend who was also now Niall's lawyer, and of course, Niall's legal guardians, the Larsens.

As if that odd mix of people wasn't enough to remind him that his son had yet another battle on his hands if he managed to recover, the uniformed police officer in the hallway guarding the door was more than enough to jog his memory.

Grace said something to Aidan's former in-laws. Judy Larsen hugged her and then she and her husband, Sam, entered the room. They headed directly toward Aidan, barely giving him time to rise from his chair before he was enveloped in yet another of their group hugs.

He was as astonished at their acceptance and support now as he had been at the parole hearing when they'd urged the board to grant him an early release. They'd told the board they were skeptical about his confession, always had been. But that even if he was guilty, they forgave him and were relieved that their daughter was no longer suffering. The fact that they were supporting him even now, and not blaming him for their grandson having almost died, humbled and shocked him.

It also shamed him that they still didn't know the full story, exactly what had happened the day their daughter died. But telling them now seemed cruel. What good would it serve?

He looked over the top of Judy Larsen's head and met Grace's worried gaze. He'd hidden the full truth from her, too. He hated lying, even by omission, especially to her. But he had to keep lying or hurt the Larsens even more.

After giving them a summary of what the doctor had

said about Niall's condition while the two of them had taken a much-needed break at their hotel down the street, he headed into the hallway.

Grace gave him a smile of encouragement and the two of them followed the others down the long hall to the conference room that the hospital administrator had lent law enforcement for their interviews. Aidan had put off answering their questions as long as he could. But with the arrival of the supervisory special agent, Grace's boss at the FBI, they couldn't be put off any longer. Especially after Aidan's probation officer told him he had no choice but to speak to them or risk violating the terms of his parole. He was so tired of the threat of returning to prison hanging over his head. But he had several more years of parole to endure.

After following Grace into the room and shutting the door behind them, Aidan turned around and stilled, shocked to see so many people there, many of them strangers. But it was the only other person dressed in a casual shirt and jeans, like him, who had his stomach dropping.

Stella. She knew—and could prove—the full truth, that one detail he wanted to keep secret above all else.

"Aidan." Grace touched his shoulder. "Over here." She led the way to two empty seats in the middle of the long table and took the one on the left for herself, leaving him to sit beside her with his lawyer, now Niall's lawyer, on his other side.

"Aidan O'Brien," Grace said, "I'd like to introduce you to Levi Perry, FBI supervisory special agent of the Knoxville field office, my boss."

Perry leaned across the table and shook Aidan's hand. "Thank you for agreeing to speak with us, Mr. O'Brien."

"Did I have a choice?"

Nate subtly nudged Aidan's foot beneath the table.

Aidan sighed. "Sorry. This isn't the best time for an interrogation with my son in the ICU."

"Interview, not interrogation," Perry corrected. "Any suspicion that fell on you early on during the investigation has been proven to be wrong. What we'd like to do now is discuss a few remaining questions we have that only you can answer. First, let me introduce you to the other people in the meeting whom you haven't met yet."

There were several higher-ups in law enforcement for the county, as well as a man in an extremely expensive-looking business suit sitting beside Perry. He was introduced as Raul Garcia, a senior member of the Tennessee Board of Probation and Parole.

Aidan stiffened. His lawyer was already pushing his chair back to stand.

"As a reminder, I'm Nathaniel Barnes, attorney for both the suspect—Niall O'Brien Larsen—and his biological father, Aidan O'Brien. If the parole board is here to consider revoking Mr. O'Brien's parole, then I must advise my client to invoke his right to remain silent. This setting isn't the proper one for that kind of discussion."

Garcia held up a hand to stop him. "I assure you, Mr. Barnes, the parole board has absolutely no intention of revoking Mr. O'Brien's parole. Consider me merely an interested observer at this time."

"I appreciate that, Mr. Garcia. But I'm still advising my client not to speak." He motioned to Aidan. "Let's go."

Aidan remained seated. "What about my son? Niall? I was told the main reason for this meeting was to get my side of what happened and any information that might help explain why Niall did what he did."

"Mitigating factors." Perry nodded. "That's why we're here, yes."

"Then I'm staying," Aidan said.

Nate slowly sat. "This is completely irregular," he grumbled. "And for the official record, I'm still advising my client to remain silent."

Perry motioned around the room. "There's no court reporter here. Nothing is being recorded or written down. There will be no official record of this meeting. And if anyone asks after we leave here today, this meeting never happened."

Aidan frowned at Nate, then Grace. "What's going on?"

She cleared her throat. "The Mystic Lake police have already provided their statements. I've given mine, as well. We've been meeting since Niall was shot, exchanging information and reviewing the evidence. Before the district attorney decides what charges to press against Niall, a barely seventeen-year-old minor, they need to know if there are any mitigating factors that should influence their decision. That's why you're here, Aidan. To speak to those factors. To speak for your son. Do you understand?"

He stared into her deep blue eyes, her words replaying in his mind. Then he glanced down the table. "Stella? Is that why you're here, too? Mitigating factors?"

She nodded. "It has to end today, Aidan. No more lies. No more cover-up. Niall's life is on the line, his future. They need to understand *everything* that went into shaping who he is, and what may have triggered him to do what he's done."

Everything. That one word sent a surge of panic through him.

Grace squeezed his forearm, recapturing his attention.

"It's time to tell us what really happened the day that Niall's biological mother died, the day that your wife, Elly O'Brien, passed away. Once everyone understands the full truth, only then can they truly understand what Niall has gone through and why he made the choices he's made."

"Mr. O'Brien," Perry began.

Aidan tuned him out and focused on Grace's beautiful face. "Did you speak to Stella already?"

"I know that she has an audio recording that she brought with her to play for us. But I haven't heard it yet."

He sighed deeply. "I can't do this."

Ignoring the potential repercussions to her career, she took his hand in hers. "The truth has been a poison inside you for years. It's been poison to Niall, too. We just didn't know that until now. Let it out, Aidan. It's the only way for everyone to truly heal. And the only way to ensure that Niall gets every chance at going home after he leaves this hospital, rather than going to a detention facility."

It was her last sentence that kept him in his chair.

"Just tell us what happened," she encouraged. "Start with the fire, then go to the day Elly passed away."

He let out a shuddering breath, and began to tell the story that had been stuck inside him for all these years. He spoke haltingly at first, stumbling over the words. But Grace took his hand again, this time beneath the table, and held on the entire time he spoke. Without that anchor, he didn't think he would have made it.

He told them about the fire at his home, finding out that his wife had run through the flames to save their son. That in spite of her burns, she'd carried him downstairs. Then a burning beam had crashed through the ceiling, breaking her spine and pinning her down, but miraculously not hitting Niall.

She'd suffered horribly, had been mostly paralyzed from the neck down and would be on a ventilator for the rest of her life, however long that was. Her parents had wanted him to stop extraordinary life-saving measures at the hospital and let her go. But he couldn't. He still had hope that she would defy the odds, prove the doctors wrong.

Months after the accident she was receiving care at home, with two nurses who rotated day shifts when he was at work or running errands. One of those nurses was Stella Simmons, now Holman. At night, Aidan was the one who took care of Elly if any alarms went off on her ventilator.

It was difficult and frustrating trying to communicate with Elly. She eventually was able to barely control one hand. But she couldn't speak, not at first anyway. Through his research online he'd discovered that a special valve could be placed in her tracheostomy that might allow her to speak once again, even though she was paralyzed.

"And it worked," he said. "I was so excited to hear what her first words would be. She didn't say 'I love you' or ask to see our son. Instead, she said, 'Let me die.'"

Perry winced across from him.

"It's what she wrote on her pad of paper, too. That same phrase. Let me die. She wanted me to end her misery. I know that some people tolerate the vent, that even paralyzed they can live fulfilling lives and still experience joy. But Elly had been so active, athletic. No amount of counseling helped her accept her condition. She was truly miserable."

He shook his head in self-disgust. "I'm the reason she suffered so long. I could have withdrawn care, signed forms at the hospital to let her die a natural death. But I was too selfish. I'd failed her by not being able to save her from the fire. I wanted to be there for her afterward, convinced my money could buy some kind of miracle cure if she could only hold on a little longer. I was a foolish man."

"Skipping to the day that she did die," Perry said. "The version of events you told the police was that you wanted to end her suffering, that you unplugged the ventilator, then waited another ten minutes until the backup battery drained. After her heart stopped, you called 911."

"That's the story I've told all these years."

"But that's not the truth, is it, Mr. O'Brien? Special Agent Grace Malone has insisted to me that you're innocent. And even your in-laws seem to believe that. Did you kill your wife?"

"What the hell does this have to do with helping my son?"

"Understanding the trauma he may have witnessed or suffered himself can help explain the decisions he's recently made. It could make all the difference in the charges pressed against him."

"I'll tell them what happened." It was Stella from the other end of the table.

"Don't," Aidan said. "Please."

"Aidan was exhausted that day, as he often was," she said, ignoring his plea. "He worked long hours and had a five-year-old son to take to day care each morning, pick up after work, feed, bathe. He could have hired a nanny but he insisted on being there for Niall, to give him as normal a life as possible even though his mother couldn't hold him or help take care of him."

Aidan squeezed his eyes shut.

Grace whispered soothing words as she continued to

hold his hand. He gripped it like a lifeline, both ashamed to be relying on her so heavily and desperate not to let go.

Stella explained that Aidan had come home, gotten the turnover report from Stella, checked on his wife, fed and bathed his son, then put him to bed. Then he'd gone out on the back deck to sit for a few minutes, to unwind, before he headed back upstairs to sit with Elly until bedtime.

"He fell asleep. It's probably the only time he ever did, fell asleep on that back deck because he was so exhausted. When he jolted awake, he realized twenty minutes had passed. He ran inside the house and upstairs to make sure his wife was still okay. He didn't hear any alarms going off on her ventilator so he thought everything would be fine. But when he went into her room, he realized everything wasn't okay."

"Mr. O'Brien." This time it was the district attorney who spoke. "I know this is an unofficial inquest, but having your wife's former nurse tell the story is still hearsay. I'd like to hear the rest from you, especially since this is a whole new version of events that I'm having trouble believing after all this time."

"It's the truth," Stella snapped. "Not a version of events. He didn't kill Elly."

"It's okay," Aidan told her, a strange sort of acceptance finally settling over him. "I've lied for years. I don't expect everyone to believe me now. But if even one person does, and it somehow helps Niall, I'll tell the rest."

He explained that when he entered the room, the first thing he noticed was that his son, who was supposed to be in bed, was playing with toy police cars and trucks by the window. The next thing he noticed was that the cord to Elly's ventilator was unplugged and that Niall was currently using it to tie up one of his so-called bad guy action figures.

The DA leaned forward. "You're saying that you didn't pull the cord on your wife's machine. Your five-year-old son did?"

Aidan nodded. "But he didn't realize what he was doing. What he'd done. I told him to grab his toys and go back to bed. I didn't want him to see what I had to do to help his mother. I plugged in the machine, called 911 and put it on speaker so I could lay her on the floor and begin doing chest compressions, CPR. But it was too late. Her backup battery had died before I came in from the porch. There were no alarms beeping. She wasn't breathing. Her heart had stopped. Nothing I did made a difference."

"When the EMTs arrived and tried to resuscitate your wife," Perry said, "they said you went to check on your son."

"I had to get out of the way so they could try to help Elly. I went to check on Niall and asked him what had happened. He was still playing with his damn cars and trucks, making beeping sounds. He said…he said mommy played with him, told him she could beep like his cars. She told him… she told him to pull the plug to make the machine go beep."

There were several sharp intakes of breath around the room.

Grace placed her hand on his shoulder. "Oh, Aidan. I'm so sorry."

The DA scoffed. "Now you're not only blaming your wife's death on your five-year-old son, you're telling us his mother essentially ended her own life. You really expect us to believe this new story?"

"Well, of course I don't expect you to believe it," Aidan bit out. "I never expected, or wanted, anyone to believe it.

It was horrific, awful. Can you imagine the pain, the absolute misery my wife felt, how desperate she was to end her suffering that she would actually convince her own child to pull the plug, knowing how that could mess him up later in life, knowing he was responsible for her death?"

He shoved his hand through his hair and tugged his other hand free from Grace to rest his forearms on top of the table. "Elly was miserable. All she asked me to do was let her go, let her die. And I was too selfish to grant her that end to her suffering. Instead, my five-year-old son did what I couldn't. He ended her pain."

The DA started to say something, but Perry stopped him. "Mr. O'Brien, if what you're saying is true, everyone in here, I'm sure, can agree that law enforcement wouldn't have done anything to punish your son. He certainly wouldn't have been prosecuted. So why did you confess to your wife's murder? What was the point?"

Aidan stared at him incredulously. "The point? Did you not hear what I said? He was a little boy. If the world heard that he'd unplugged that machine, that knowledge would have followed him the rest of his life. People can be cruel, horrible to each other. Parents would have talked. Their children would have heard. They'd have teased and bullied him at school. As it is, his grandparents had to move several hours away to raise him because of kids teasing him over his father killing his mother. I made a split-second decision to protect my son, choosing the lesser of evils. I believed it was far better for him to grow up thinking his father was an evil monster than to realize he'd inadvertently killed his own mother. That's why I confessed. To try to spare him that kind of pain. But even more than that, I was, in my own misguided way, trying to protect Elly, and the Larsens."

"Your wife and her parents?" Perry asked. "Please explain what you mean by that."

A single tear slid down Aidan's cheek. He angrily wiped it away. "Elly loved Niall more than anything. He was her world. If she'd been in her right frame of mind, not blinded by the agony of a life she couldn't accept, she never would have tricked him into doing what he did. She wouldn't want that guilt later in life to eat at his soul. And I didn't want her parents or friends to ever know that she'd done something that would have shamed her. So, as strange as it may seem to someone not in that situation, yes, I confessed to protect both my wife's reputation and my son. At the time, I felt my life was over anyway. And that because I refused to help her, I deserved my fate. Prison. But after seeing what's become of Niall, how tortured he was to discover his father confessed to his mother's murder, I wonder if he'd have been better off knowing the truth from the beginning."

"That brings us to those mitigating circumstances," Perry said. "If we take what you just said as fact—"

"There's no proof," the DA said, looking extremely skeptical.

"Assume it's a fact for now. What the Larsens told us earlier is that when five year-old Niall was told that his mother was dead, that he'd never see her again, he shut down. He was never able to answer questions about anything he saw that day because his mind blanked out his memories. But it must have simmered below the surface because he suffered night terrors for years. And he acted out, had all kinds of behavioral issues. His grandparents became desperate to help him. They'd kept in touch with one of his nurses, Stella Simmons, who is now Stella Holman, because they'd grown close in the months that Stella helped care for their daughter. When they asked for recommendations, Stella helped them find a child psychiatrist. And she took him to his sessions whenever the Larsens couldn't."

Perry looked around the table as if to make sure that everyone was paying attention. "Let's skip ahead to the year before Mr. O'Brien's parole hearing. The Larsens said that Niall as a fifteen-year-old at the time became curious to learn about his father. It didn't take much internet searching to find out everything that the media had reported. He believed his father killed his mother. And it ate at him. He sent Mr. O'Brien hate mail and in response, Mr. O'Brien had his lawyer contact them to let them know that Niall needed help."

Barnes spoke up to add a lawyer's viewpoint to the discussion. "Obviously, Niall O'Brien has been through trauma in his young life even if he's never had a clear memory of what happened. Finding out disturbing things about his father sent him over the edge. He came up with a plan to have his father sent back to prison where he felt he belonged. He'd heard about the Crossbow Killer on the news and decided to try to frame Aidan as the killer. An adult, especially those of us in law enforcement, would of course know that framing someone isn't nearly as easy as Niall thought it would be. When his actions didn't achieve the results he wanted, he became desperate, doing what he could to hurt his father. But I contend that he wasn't specifically trying to hurt anyone else. He only wanted to hurt Mr. O'Brien."

"Hold it, hold it," the DA said. "I'm one of the ones who didn't hear from Mrs. Holman in the meetings you've been having, or from the Larsens. What exactly did they testify to at the parole hearing that you mentioned earlier? If it's more of this unsubstantiated new story that O'Brien is putting forth, I don't see where any of that is relevant and will help the younger O'Brien avoid the charges I'm inclined to levy against him."

"They found out the truth," Aidan said, his voice gruff with anger. "They testified that they knew that Niall had pulled the plug, not me. I didn't ask them to speak on my behalf. I didn't want them to. But they did."

"Sounds convenient."

Aidan glared at him. "Convenient? Why the hell do you think my wife's parents would lie to a parole board? You think they'd want their daughter's killer out of prison? If you think that, you're an idiot."

The DA pointed at Aidan. "Now you listen here—"

"Don't you dare speak to him that way." Stella stood, her expression one of loathing as she addressed the district attorney. "*You* listen. All of you. Aidan didn't come here today willingly to tell his story. He came because his parole officer ordered him to, and because all of you asked him. Enough people know bits and pieces about the truth to have pieced it together even though he has tried for years to keep it quiet. As to whether what he's saying is true or not, I've got proof that it is. I brought a recording I'd like to play for all of you that—"

"Stella," Aidan rasped. "Don't. Leave it alone."

"I'm sorry, Aidan. But Grace was right when she said this has been a poison in your soul, and that it's poison to Niall as well, whether he realizes it or not. The only antidote to that poison is the truth."

He shoved to his feet. "Then you'll do it without me." He strode out the door.

"Aiden, wait." Grace followed him into the hallway and shut the door behind her.

He turned and she wrapped her arms around his waist, hugging him tight. Unable to stop himself, even though he knew he should, he hugged her tighter and rested his cheek on the top of her head. Some of the pain and anger inside him melted away at the feel of her in his arms. She was the embodiment of kindness, of empathy, of caring. And he selfishly drew strength from her, even at the risk of someone seeing them.

The convict and the FBI agent.

A father with a murderous son and a woman dedicated to justice.

It could never work.

And even if, by some miracle, there was some way for them to be together, he'd made a mess of things with his son. Niall had to be his first priority now. Somehow he had to fix the damage he'd caused by trying to cover everything up in the first place.

Regret ate at him as he pulled away. "Go back inside. I'm sure they're waiting for you."

"Where are you going?" she asked.

"To see the Larsens. They deserve to know the truth before someone else tells them."

"Do you want me to go with you?"

He stared at her in wonder. "You're amazing, you know that?" Unable to resist the impulse, he feathered his hand down the side of her face, then pressed a soft kiss against her lips. "Thank you. But I need to do this myself." He quickly turned and strode away.

Chapter Twenty-One

Grace remained in the hospital conference room long after everyone else had left. She was still reeling from listening to the recording that Stella had secretly made during one of Niall's visits to the child psychiatrist. It was both shocking and sickening to listen to the sweet, innocent voice of an eight-year-old child speaking under the influence of hypnosis. Without any true understanding about what he revealed, he'd walked the doctor and Stella as his guardian during that visit through everything that happened the day that his mother died.

And everything he said corroborated what Aidan had said.

Elly O'Brien had taken her own life with her son's help, using him to pull the plug while Aidan was out of the room.

Stella had explained that Elly likely heard the sound of the back door and knew that her husband had gone outside. Since he'd already checked on her and confirmed that her machine was functioning properly, there was no reason he shouldn't have felt secure stepping out for a few minutes. Even if he hadn't fallen asleep, at any other time on any other day the odds of anything bad happening to Elly while he was outside for only twenty minutes were very low. But the stars had aligned for Elly and she got her deepest, darkest wish—release from a life she considered to be unbearable.

At the expense of her five-year-old little boy and her husband.

It broke Grace's heart that Elly had been so miserable as to do that. And it broke her heart that Aidan knew and had taken on the guilt, and punishment, for not helping her and making her believe she had no other choice. Their beautiful little family had been irrevocably destroyed the day of the fire in their home, though none of them had realized it at the time.

But that wasn't the only thing on Grace's mind, or the only reason she was still sitting in the empty conference room trying to gather her thoughts and emotions. She was also reeling over the final conclusion presented by Mr. Garcia, the probation board member. He was going to meet with the rest of the board and recommend that they provide the governor with Aidan's name as someone who should be pardoned. Not just pardoned, but fully exonerated, his record expunged and all of his rights restored—including the cancellation of his parole.

It would take months, maybe longer, for all the red tape to be cut and the legal pieces set into place. But Aidan would have what he deserved: complete exoneration. The world would know he was innocent. It was what Grace had wanted all along. But now that it was being granted, she wasn't sure the cost was worth it.

Aidan had spent ten long years in prison to protect his son, Elly and the Larsens. Now the truth would all come out and they'd have to face the consequences. Everything he'd worked so hard for all this time was being nullified.

And she couldn't help but worry what more that might cost him. She already knew what it had cost her.

Her career.

She looked down at the white envelope in her hands, given to her by her boss. It was official notice that she was being fired, effective immediately. It had been printed out before he'd even come to Chattanooga to meet with her. She was being let go because of unprofessional conduct and poor judgment in the execution of her duties. The team she'd worked with back in the Knoxville field office would go on to investigate and solve the Crossbow Killer case without her. That alone had her feeling empty inside. She'd so hoped that the anonymous tip that had her sent to Mystic Lake would have resulted in her leading the charge and solving the case. That would have been a major step up in her career. Instead, it had ended her career.

Opening the envelope, she pulled out the picture that her boss had included with the termination papers, a picture that had been snapped of her and Aidan kissing outside her room at the B and B after they'd returned from help-lessly watching his cabin burn to the ground. The reporter they'd both thought was asleep in her room must have heard them and opened her door just enough to take that picture. And when she'd leaked the story about the Crossbow Killer supposedly in Mystic Lake, she'd included that picture of the FBI agent in town getting a little too friendly with the town's only parolee—a man who'd confessed to the murder of his wife. There was no coming back from that, even though Aidan had now been proven innocent, unofficially at least. At the time the picture was taken, he was still a convicted murderer with no hope of that ever changing.

Sighing heavily, she slid the picture back into the envelope and stood. As she grabbed her jacket off the back of her chair, she automatically felt for her holster to make sure it was in place. But she didn't have her holster or her gun anymore. She'd had to turn them over to her boss along with her FBI credentials and the Bureau's credit card. She'd even had to turn over her car keys so he could commandeer her FBI vest inside it and her laptop and files before he had the rental company retrieve the SUV.

She winced when she remembered the hole in the back of it from the arrow. But that was her former employer's problem now. As it was, they'd left her without any transportation. She'd have to arrange for another rental just to get back to her room at Mystic Lake to retrieve her personal belongings.

It had been nearly a decade since she'd first started her career as a beat cop before becoming a special agent. Without a gun, she felt naked, lost. She had absolutely no idea how to live life as a civilian.

Thankfully, she had a generous severance package that her boss had fought for due to her pristine service record prior to this fiasco at Mystic Lake. And she had her savings to fall back on. But neither of those would last forever. She needed to figure out what she was going to do with the rest of her life.

Before she left the hospital, she stopped in the ICU to check on Niall and his family. She hadn't expected Aidan to be there, and he wasn't. He was in another conference room of the hospital being briefed by his lawyer about everything that had happened after he'd walked out of the meeting.

The Larsens had red-rimmed eyes from crying, no doubt because they now knew just how horribly their daughter had suffered and the disastrous chain of events she'd unwittingly put into motion. But they were strong, relying on their faith to get them through. After she spoke to them for several minutes, they shared a prayer for Niall and Aidan. And it puts tears in Grace's eyes when they added her name in their prayer, as well.

She hugged them one last time and said her goodbyes. Then she headed downstairs to wait for her rental car to arrive.

Over an hour later, she emerged from the twisty, narrow road through the mountains into downtown Mystic Lake. She stopped at the Main Street parking lot, stunned to see thick black smoke rising from the trees off to her right, in the direction of the marina, and the sound of sirens as the fire department and police responded. She almost headed in that direction to offer help, but then she remembered she wasn't law enforcement anymore. She was a regular civilian and didn't even have the authority to direct traffic.

Instead, she drove around the end of the lake to the B and B and parked out back. Hopefully, Aidan would return soon. She really needed to talk to him, to see how he was doing, and maybe even feel around about where he saw his future heading. Right now her own future was both bleak and wide-open with possibilities.

She sincerely hoped one of those possibilities was Aidan.

As she stepped out of her car, another car pulled into the empty slot beside hers. She smiled a greeting at the man driving, then rounded the back of his car to head to the B and B.

He got out as she was passing him and smiled. "Heard you were looking for me."

She stopped in confusion. "I'm sorry, I don't—"

He pointed toward his car.

She glanced through the rear window. There on the back seat was a large crossbow and a quiver of arrows, with large white feathers attached to each of them. She whirled around to run. An explosion of white-hot pain slammed against the side of her head. Everything went dark.

Chapter Twenty-Two

Aidan swerved to avoid a pothole as he navigated the long narrow road to Mystic Lake. When he'd set out a few days ago down this road, he'd been pushing his truck as fast as it could go on his way to the hospital. This time, he took the road at a more sane speed, and was actually, for the first time in a long time, enjoying the gorgeous views of the mountains and trees as he went. And he was smiling.

It was as if he'd come out of a long dark tunnel where he'd been living since the day of the fire that so horribly injured his wife. Today, everything had turned around. The truth, the full truth, was out. And what had happened once all the key people knew that truth had blown him away.

The Larsens had been sad, but not entirely surprised to hear that Elly had essentially orchestrated her own death. And they forgave him for keeping the truth from them. More importantly, they forgave him for not manning up and helping Elly when she needed him the most. They were thankful he'd never taken on that burden and hoped he could finally move on and be happy.

The DA, after listening to the recording of Niall as a little boy saying what he'd done, conferred with Chief Dawson and others and they agreed not to press charges against

Niall as long as he received extensive counseling to help him overcome the trauma of his past. And that his record remained clean for the next two years.

Then Garcia, the parole board member, had stated he would work with the rest of the board and the governor to pursue having Aidan's record expunged and a full pardon and restoration of Aidan's rights.

An emergency meeting had been held just an hour ago. When Aidan's lawyer came out, he was grinning from ear to ear. He told Aidan that the governor and the parole board had heard enough today to immediately grant him an end to his parole. Everything else, expunging his record and spreading the news that he wasn't guilty, would take time. But Aidan didn't even care about all of that. What he cared about was that he was now free, truly free. He never had to face a probation officer again. And he could hunt with a gun in the future like anyone else, assuming he ever bought a gun. He was so used to hunting with a bow and arrow that he didn't know if he'd ever favor any other weapon.

But the best gift of all today was that his son had been weaned out of the medically induced coma and finally opened his eyes. Aidan had agreed with the Larsens that he shouldn't be there when it was done. Niall would need to be carefully updated on everything that had happened. It could take a while for him to let go of the hate and accept the truth. Until then, his adoptive parents and his court-appointed psychiatrist would help him. And one day, hopefully soon, a family reunion with Aidan would be in the cards.

He grinned and drove past Main Street, then slowed, frowning as he noted dark smoke in the sky far out of town, possibly near the marina. Whatever was happening, he hoped no one was hurt and that the fire was put out quickly.

Continuing on, he headed around back of the B and B, looking forward to talking to Grace and updating her about everything that had happened. Hell, he might even ask her on a date to celebrate. Wouldn't that be something? To be with her and not worry about anyone's opinions? After all, her boss had been in the meeting and agreed that Aidan was completely innocent. All of that time being so careful around her had been worth it. Her career was salvaged and now there was nothing standing in the way of expressing their intense attraction to each other. Heck, attraction was a paltry term and did nothing to describe the all-consuming need he had for her and vice versa. For the first time in years he was looking forward to his future. And more than anything, he wanted Grace Malone to be a part of that future.

If she would have him.

As he parked, he was disappointed that he didn't see her rental SUV in the lot. The Larsens had told him that Grace was going to the B and B when she left. She must have stopped off somewhere else, maybe a store back in Chattanooga. Or maybe she was helping with whatever was going on down at the marina.

He parked and pulled out his phone to call Chief Dawson as he exited his truck.

"Hey, Aidan," the chief said, sounding out of breath. "We're kind of busy out here. What do you need?"

"The marina? Is that where the smoke's coming from?"

"You guessed it. One of the boats blew up and is on fire. We're helping the fire department move other boats nearby to try to keep the fire from spreading."

"Injuries?"

"None, thank God. Sorry to be short, but why did you call?"

"Grace. I don't see her SUV in the B and B parking lot—"

"Didn't you hear? She doesn't have that SUV anymore. Her boss turned it back in when he fired her."

Aidan stopped by the last car in the lot. "What did you say? He fired her?"

"Oh, man. Sorry you heard it this way. She can explain when you see her."

He didn't need an explanation. The only reason Grace would have lost her job was him. He swore. "All right. Thanks. Do you happen to know what she's driving now?"

"No idea. Gotta go. It's all law enforcement hands on deck, all four of us." He laughed. "Your lawyer informed me about your parole being canceled. Congratulations on how things worked out. Enjoy your freedom, Aidan. You deserve it." The line clicked, ending the call.

Aidan's earlier euphoria was gone. In its place was a sim-mering anger at both Grace's boss and himself. He should have been more careful. Destroying her career was the last thing he'd wanted. He'd have to talk to his lawyer to see if there was something they could do to force the FBI to reinstate her. But right now he couldn't imagine what that might be.

He headed into the B and B. After a brief stop to make sure that Stella knew he harbored no ill feelings toward her and appreciated her good intentions, he hurried upstairs and knocked on Grace's door. After several knocks and several minutes of waiting, he jogged downstairs and sought out Stella again. But she hadn't seen Grace.

One of the customers in the restaurant overheard them

and said he was walking into the restaurant when he noticed Grace pulling up in the parking lot. As far as he knew, she'd never come inside, but she could have and he just didn't notice.

"Do you remember which car was hers?" Aidan asked.

"Yeah, one of those smaller cars. A four-door, white. Toyota I think. I was surprised because she normally drives a big SUV."

"Thanks." Aidan strode outside to the parking lot. He remembered passing a white Toyota and easily found it again amid the trucks and Jeeps in the lot. An uneasy feeling tingled down his spine as he peered into her car. Nothing looked out of place. The car was locked and all of the windows were rolled up. It simply looked as if she'd parked and gone inside.

But she hadn't.

So where was she?

He circled the car, looking for anything that might tell him what was going on. The small shoe prints outside the driver's door looked to be about her size. She must have gotten out of the car. The prints went around the back of another car and then…other prints converged on hers. They were large, the size of a man probably as big as Aidan. And the prints trampled over the top of Grace's. After that, the man's prints deepened in the dirt and gravel. But there were no more prints from Grace.

To anyone else, what had happened here might not be obvious. But to Aidan, who'd been tracking game almost daily for well over a year now, they were a glaring neon sign telling him something had happened to Grace. Something bad.

The car where her prints ended didn't appear to be the

car that was parked here now. This car was a large SUV and was parked on some of those prints, which meant they were there before the SUV pulled in. So the man who'd scuffled with Grace had taken off in his own car. And Aidan didn't doubt for a minute that he'd taken Grace with him, against her will.

A bead of sweat rolled down his back in spite of the chill in the air as he whipped out his phone and called Dawson again. He walked back to Grace's car and slowly circled it, looking for other clues.

"Aidan," Dawson said, "I can't talk right now. I'm trying to dock a boat that—"

"It's Grace. She's been abducted."

"What the... Are you sure? Tell me what happened."

Aidan explained the situation, the clues as he continued to slowly inspect the ground around her car. When he reached the right front tire, he bellowed in fury. "He's got her, Dawson. That animal has her."

"Who? Calm down. Tell me what's going on."

Aidan bent down to inspect the arrow sticking out of Grace's tire, an arrow with a large white feather hanging from the end.

"The Crossbow Killer. The real one. He's here, in Mystic Lake. And he's got Grace."

Dawson swore viciously. "How much do you want to bet the fire at the marina was his doing, a diversion?" He yelled for Fletcher and Collier, shouting commands as he transferred responsibility for the marina scene to Ortiz to continue working with the firefighters.

Aidan followed the clues from the other car left in the gravel and noted the direction it had taken. Then he ran to his truck and jumped in.

"All right," Dawson said. "We're heading to our cars now. We'll meet you at the B and B and—"

"Forget the B and B." He raced his truck out of the parking lot, slowing to determine which way the other vehicle's distinctive tire tracks had gone. Then he made the turn and gunned the engine.

"Wait, why?" Dawson demanded. "Talk to me."

"He's in a Jeep, older model, four-wheel drive. I don't know the color. I'm judging by the tracks, the width of the wheel base. The tires are muddy. The tracks are fresh, so I've got something to follow. They're running parallel with the lake so far, heading out of town."

Dawson shouted orders over his radio to the others. "Older model Jeep heading northwest, parallel with the lake. Be on the lookout."

"Trace her phone, Dawson. See if you can get a bead on it. I don't want to call it in case the ringer is on and it alerts the guy, assuming she even has it at this point. He may have tossed it."

"Will do." He spoke into his radio to Fletcher, telling her to put a trace on Malone's phone. "And contact the FBI. Even if they don't give a damn about their own agent anymore, they should at least want to get their butts up here to help us find that killer they're all hot and bothered about."

Aidan suddenly slammed his brakes, fishtailing across the gravel road. He engaged the four-wheel drive on his truck and quickly backed up. Then he turned where the Jeep had turned and slowed to look for more signs of it passing this way.

"Give me an update, O'Brien. I'm four minutes out. Where am I going?"

"Old logging trail. He's heading up the mountain."

"By Jesper's hunting cabin, the one that's falling down?"

"That's the one. Wait. Ah, hell." He slammed his brakes again and slid to a halt, then leaped from his truck.

"What, O'Brien? Talk to me."

"The Jeep. I found it. Empty. He ditched it, a quarter mile up the road." Aidan ran back to his truck and flipped the seat forward. He pulled out his bow and an arrow and strapped the quiver of extra arrows over his neck and shoulder to let it hang out of the way. Squatting down, he searched the dirt until he picked up two sets of shoe prints leading deeper into the trees. "I've got their trail. Heading almost due west up the mountain through the woods. I'll mark an X in the dirt to help you find it, about ten feet off the right side of the road. I'm hanging up now, but you can do something fancy to track my cell to keep up with me."

"No, Aidan. Stay on the line. Wait for us. We'll be there in less than three minutes, coming in hot."

"To hell with that. Every minute she's alone with him is one minute too long."

"What are you going to do? You don't even have a gun."

He notched an arrow in his bow. "I'm hunting the Crossbow Killer."

Chapter Twenty-Three

He shoved Grace in the back, making her stumble and almost fall on the leaf-strewn forest floor.

"Hurry up," he told her.

She glared at him over her shoulder.

He laughed.

"What do you want from me? If you're really the Crossbow Killer, you would have killed me in the parking lot. Abducting people isn't what he does."

"He, as in I, don't miss what I aim at either, like that idiot you cops arrested. I'm smart enough to attach the feathers to my bows after I take down my target instead of letting the arrow fly wherever it wants because of a feather dragging it down, like that kid you've been giving credit for my hard work. Oh, and I don't burn down cabins, either. Although now that I think of it, that could be fun, setting the woods on fire and watching an entire mountain burn." He shoved her again. "Keep moving. And show some respect or I'll end this right here."

"Where are we going? I can make better time if you tell me our destination."

He suddenly jerked her to a stop. "Oh, man. This is definitely new territory for me, taking a living victim. Your phone's on, isn't it? You've got an open mic, an open call and you're trying to get me to give up our location. Hand it over."

"I don't have it. I left it in my car."

He backhanded her, whirling her around. She fell against a tree, biting her lip to keep from giving him the satisfaction of crying out. The metallic taste of blood filled her mouth.

"Phone," he demanded. "Now."

She was about to lie again and say she didn't have it, anything to stall for time, to give someone a chance to trace her line. But suddenly the arrow was pointing directly at her head. He couldn't miss from three feet away, especially since he'd admitted he attached his feathers after shooting the arrows. He really did know what he was doing, which meant he was even more skilled and deadly than she thought. She pulled out her cell phone and handed it to him.

He dropped it to the ground and stomped on it until it crunched into little pieces. His lips curled in a sneer as he kept the arrow pointed at her. "Now move. Straight ahead. Hurry."

As much as possible, she tried to slow them down without being too obvious. She carefully stepped over fallen logs, skirted farther around bushes than necessary. And the entire time she scanned the woods around them, searching for something, anything or anyone to give her a chance to escape.

Had her former boss received the call she'd speed dialed in her pocket? Was he even still in the area where he could help her? She hoped he was, and that help was on the way. But she had to assume the worst, that she was on her own. She'd been trained in hand-to-hand combat, trained to try to outthink an opponent who was bigger than her or had her outgunned. There had to be a way out of this. All she had to do was find it.

The distant sound of gurgling water caught her attention. A waterfall? Or something man-made like an outdoor shower? How could she use it to her advantage?

He shoved her again, almost making her fall. "Quit stalling. I don't have time for this. I need to make my statement and get out of here before they figure out where I am."

She stopped and looked over her shoulder. "What kind of statement are you—"

This time he hit her with the bow, the arrow's razor-sharp edge slicing across her hand. She gasped at the fiery pain and grabbed the wound, pressing it hard to try to stop the bleeding.

"Move," he gritted out, holding up the bow again, the now bloody arrow less than a foot from her face.

She whirled around and hurried forward. His words kept running through her mind. He wanted to make a statement. And he'd complained about someone else taking credit for his work. Niall. He must have heard the media reports and come to Mystic Lake. He clearly didn't want someone else being labeled the Crossbow Killer. That distinction was entirely his. And he was here to prove it. To make a statement. How does a killer make a statement?

He kills.

Which meant he was definitely planning to kill her, but he apparently had a specific place in mind to do it. He was in a hurry to reach his destination and do what he'd planned. Knowing she'd had her phone on didn't change their direction. It only had him pressing her to hurry.

They were close, then. Had to be. Close to wherever his statement was going to take place. Which meant it was go time. She had to make a run for it. But she was bleeding, and wearing soft leather shoes that didn't grip the ground, not the kind of hard-soled hiking boots he had on. He was bigger, taller, with longer strides. And he was armed. How was she going to make a run for it with any real hope of getting away and not being shot?

Think, Grace. Think.

The sound of the water was getting closer, louder.

"Hurry."

She sped up. She was definitely hearing a waterfall. She'd studied the area on topographical maps before coming here, wanting to be sure she understood the main landmarks as well as the more dangerous areas to avoid. When she'd woken up in his Jeep, Mystic Lake had been on their right, barely visible through the trees. That meant they'd headed north. Then he'd turned left, west, up a dirt road, past a ramshackle cabin that had seen better days. A picture formed in her mind with the little Xs that marked areas for hikers on the local tourism map she'd gotten while in Chattanooga before going to Mystic Lake.

The old logging trail. That was where they'd gone. Which meant they were heading toward the marina. And toward Mystic Falls. Yes, that was what she heard. A waterfall. If only she could reach it before he did and find the path marked on the map, she might be able to take the upper loop above the falls. And maybe somehow she could fool him into thinking she'd taken the easier, downhill loop. It wasn't much of an escape plan, but it might give her a chance to put some distance between them.

It was better than nothing.

She sped up some more, searching the ground for what she'd need to try to fool him.

"Hey," he called out, "wait up."

She moved faster, then ducked down and grabbed a handful of small rocks from the trail and quickly tucked them into her jacket pocket.

A whistle of air sounded as something shot past her so fast and close she didn't have time to duck. She stumbled to a halt as she stared at the haft of an arrow buried in the tree a few feet in front of her. It had only missed her by a fraction of an inch. Her lungs seized in her chest and she started to shake.

He grabbed her shoulder and whirled her around, slamming her against a tree. His mouth curled back like a rabid animal, revealing his teeth. But it was his eyes that sent a burst of terror straight through her. They were so dark they were almost black. And there wasn't an ounce of humanity in them. All she saw was rage and bloodlust, a thirst to kill that was being kept in check by the barest thread.

"Do that again, try to run, and the next one goes in your brain." He shook her. "Got it?"

"Got...got it. No running."

"Move. It's almost over." He shoved her forward.

She drew a shaky breath, then another as she forced her feet to keep moving. He was going to kill her. No doubt about it. But if that was going to happen, it would be on her terms. No way would she meekly march to her death and let him choose just when he was going to shoot her. The upper loop above the falls was the only way, her only chance to at least try to put some distance between them. Maybe she'd get lucky and he'd fall over the waterfall to the rocky floor below.

Or maybe she'd end up with an arrow in her back.

She pictured the falls in her mind, the trails she'd studied on the map. The sound and smell of the water signaled they were almost there. Her possibly only chance at survival was coming, and she had to take it, no matter how terrified she was. Fighting him wasn't an option. She'd lose in that scenario. Flight was her only choice. She'd have to run as if her life depended on it.

Because it did.

A mist began to rise in the woods up ahead. No doubt it must be that time of day that had helped to give Mystic Lake its name, as well as the Smoky Mountains. It was a phenomenon of the climate, like little puffs of smoke moving in and making it harder to see.

"Just a little farther," he yelled behind her. "When we get to the falls, turn right, head down toward the lake."

"Okay," she called back, carefully pulling the rocks out of her pocket without making any sudden moves that would give her away.

Suddenly, the mist deepened, obscuring her view. She hesitated.

"Turn right," he called out.

She hurled the rocks off to the right, hoping he'd hear them and think that was her stumbling down the path. Then she took off to her left, as quietly as possible, up the trail toward the top of the falls. She was about to turn onto the loop that she'd seen on the map when he shouted from farther down the path. He must have already realized she'd gone the other way.

Pushing herself forward, she struggled against the incline. She could hear footsteps somewhere behind her as he struggled up the same incline, swearing at her and promising death.

"This way," a voice called out, a woman's voice. "Grace, over here."

A hand reached out of the mist and yanked her into the trees just before an arrow shot past her, so close she could feel its heat.

"Run," the woman told her, pointing to a break in the trees. "That way. Aidan's coming for you."

Grace didn't stop to ask who she was or why she was there. She grabbed for her hand as she ran past to pull the woman with her. But instead of grabbing flesh and blood her hand went through mist.

The sound of the killer's footsteps zipping past her up the loop galvanized her into action. She ran in the direction the woman had told her, back the way they'd come but on a slightly different path. Mist swirled around her as she ran and she would have sworn that somehow the rough terrain smoothed out, almost as if she were running so fast she was taking flight.

She was hallucinating. She had to be. And where was that woman who'd helped her? Grace slowed. She had to go back. She couldn't leave someone behind with a killer out here.

"Aidan, over here!"

Grace stumbled to a halt, startled to hear the woman calling out to Aidan in a voice that sounded like her own.

"Aidan!" the woman called again from the mist.

"Grace!"

It was Aidan's voice, somewhere up ahead.

"Aidan! Here! I'm here!" Grace ran forward, stumbled and fell, then leaped back up and ran again. "Aidan!"

"Grace! I'm coming!" His footsteps pounded on the earth up ahead.

Swearing sounded behind her along with the pounding of footsteps in pursuit. The killer was closing in. A bubble of hysteria rose in Grace's throat.

"Aidan, he's behind me! He's got a crossbow!" A sob caught in her chest, both from the terror of the man closing in from behind and the terror that the one she was running to was in the path of his arrow.

"Look out, Aidan!" she cried out.

"Grace, drop! Now!"

She dived to the forest floor.

The zing of arrows slicing through the air whipped over-head. A loud, gurgling scream sounded through the forest, sending a cloud of birds to flight above the trees. She lay there, afraid to move. Afraid she'd be shot if she did. And even more terrified to find out who had made that horrible gurgling sound.

Suddenly, Aidan was on his knees in front of her, scoop-ing her onto his lap, his brow lined with worry as he ran his hands over her, apparently searching for injuries. "Grace, my God. Are you okay? Your hand—"

"The shooter, he's back there, in the mist." She looked behind her. "Where? Where is he?"

Aidan gently turned her head to look at him. "You don't need to see that. He won't hurt you, or anyone else, ever again."

"I don't… How did you see him? The mist is so—"

"What mist?" He ran his fingers through her hair, over her scalp. "Did you hit your head?"

"Did I…no… I mean, yes, he knocked me out but then—"

"We need to get you to the hospital." He stood with her cradled against his chest, his bow and arrows hanging from straps across his shoulders as he headed back in the direction he'd come from.

Grace clung to him and peered over his shoulder. "I don't understand. It was such a thick mist, a fog. If it hadn't rolled in I couldn't have gotten away. Where did it go?"

"We'll wrap that hand as soon as I get you to my truck. I've got a first-aid kit inside."

"Aidan, we have to go back. That woman...we have to find her. She showed me the path to take. She saved my life."

He stopped and looked down at her. "Grace, there's no one else out here."

"But there is!" she insisted. "She called your name. Didn't you hear her?"

He shook his head, looking even more concerned. "I only heard you. Come on. Let's get you to a doctor." He took off again, insisting on carrying her in spite of her insistence that she could walk.

The sound of more voices, familiar ones, came from up ahead. The Mystic Lake police.

"Over here," Aidan called out. "I've got her. She's hurt."

"I'm fine," she assured him. "It's just a scratch."

"And a huge knot on your head. I swear I'm going to have to wrap you in bubble wrap after this." He hurried toward the sounds of the others crashing through the woods toward them.

Grace gave up trying to explain to him that she really was okay. She looked over his shoulder. The mist was back again, in the distance. And as she watched, the outline of a woman formed, with a beautiful smiling face. A face that Grace recognized from the picture that Aidan had saved from the cabin fire.

Elly O'Brien.

Chapter Twenty-Four

Grace stood at the end of the dock, looking out at the clear blue waters of Mystic Lake. It was beautiful here, and sometimes deadly. But it could be magical and miraculous, too. She was living proof of that.

The investigation into the Crossbow Killer had shown that when he'd abducted her six months ago, he'd first abducted someone else, a tourist passing through. He'd killed her in his usual way, with his crossbow and that showy white and red feather fluttering on the end of an arrow. And he'd laid her out on the ground at the bottom of the falls for the next tourist in the area to discover. His plan had apparently been to place Grace beside the other woman. Two kills in one day. He'd wanted to shock the world and turn all of the attention back to him instead of to Niall.

Thankfully, his plan hadn't worked. And now the world knew him for what he really was—a twisted sociopath with no excuses for any of the evil he'd done. Twenty-eight-year-old John Smith had a background as vanilla as his name. He was a single man working as a low-level manager in an office supply store. He'd had an average, uneventful childhood with supportive parents. There was no evidence that he was ever abused. He wasn't bullied in school. The most the FBI had been able to piece together was that he'd resented being so…average. And that he'd begun his reign of terror to get attention, to make himself appear as something more than he was—just an average forgettable man.

She shivered and shook her head. What a waste of life, both his and all of the people he'd hurt and killed. But it was over now. He'd never hurt anyone else again.

Warm, strong hands wrapped around her waist and pulled her back against an impressively muscled chest, making her sigh with pleasure. Aidan.

He nuzzled her ear and kissed the side of her neck before straightening. "Are you out here in the hopes that you'll see Elly again?"

"Do you finally believe me about what happened that day?"

"I believe you believe. Isn't that enough? You did have a concussion, you know."

"I like my version better, that Elly stuck around this world long enough to make sure that her little family was taken care of."

He hugged her tighter and leaned over to give her another kiss, this one along the side of her jaw. "You're the one who saved our family, Grace Malone O'Brien. If it wasn't for you, I'd still be living in that deep dark shell where I'd been merely existing for so many years. And there's no telling what would have happened to Niall. He's doing amazingly well now." Aidan slid his hand down her slightly rounding belly. "And he's looking forward to welcoming a new sister or brother in the summer, about the time our cabin is finally finished being rebuilt and we can move out of this rental."

She smiled and turned around.

He winced and adjusted her shoulder holster. "I like you

better without a gun to dig into me when I hug you. Why do you have your uniform on? You don't start the new job until tomorrow."

"I wanted to make sure everything fit just right. And when I saw the sparkling water out the window, I couldn't resist a quick walk down to the dock before changing back into my regular clothes."

"Are you sure you really want to go back to work? You know you don't have to. We don't need the money."

"I've tried the 'staying at home while my husband is in his office working all day' routine. That's not my idea of fun."

"If you want your job back with the FBI, you know that Nate is confident he can force them to re-hire you."

"You're so sweet, always wanting to slay my dragons for me. But the FBI never felt like home, not like Mystic Lake does. Besides, why would I want a job that would take me away from you for large spans of time?"

He gently feathered her hair back from her face. "You shouldn't have to give up your dreams. Let me fix this for you, give you back your special agent career."

"Oh, Aidan. You've already given me everything I can possibly want. You." She pressed a soft kiss against his lips. "As for my career, it's going exactly where I needed it to go. I just didn't realize it when I started out. I can make a real difference here. Dawson and the team need me. So does Mystic Lake. Our population is growing little by little. The police force has to grow right along with it."

He grinned. "Our population is definitely growing." He pressed a hand against her belly again. "By one. For now."

She slid her arms up his chest. "For now? How many little O'Briens are you wanting, Mr. O'Brien?"

"What I really want right now is you. And since this is our last day of vacation together before you start your new job, I was hoping we could spend most of the day indoors."

She grinned up at him. "Oh really? And what do you plan to do if we're both closed up in the cabin all day?"

He gave her an answering smile and scooped her up in his arms, cradling her against his chest. "I plan to love you, Grace. Always. Today and every day for the rest of our lives."

She sighed happily and locked her arms behind his neck. "And I'll love you right back, Aidan. Forever and always."

He kissed her, a gentle touch of the lips that told her more than words ever could just how much he cherished her. But the kiss quickly changed, becoming hotter and more wild until they both broke apart, breathless and dazed.

"Aidan, if you don't get me inside, fast, I'm going to start shedding my clothes right here and completely shock the neighbors."

He grinned and took off running toward the house with her laughing the whole way there.

* * * * *

Look for more books in Lena Diaz's
Mystic Lake miniseries coming soon
from Harlequin Intrigue!

Harlequin® Reader Service

Enjoyed your book?

Try the perfect subscription for Romance readers and get more great books like this delivered right to your door.

See why over 10+ million readers have tried Harlequin Reader Service.

Start with a Free Welcome Collection with free books and a gift—valued over $20.

Choose any series in print or ebook. See website for details and order today:

TryReaderService.com/subscriptions

RSBPA2409